Also by June J. McInerney

Fiction
Forty-Thirty
Rainbow in the Sky
Cats of Nine Tales
The Basset Chronicles
Adventures of Oreigh Ogglefont

Non-Fiction
Meditations for New Members

Poetry Collections
Spinach Water
Exodus Ending

Musicals
We Three Kings
Noah's Rainbow
Beauty and the Beast
Peter, the Wolf, and Red Riding Hood

To Naduna~
Thank you! Enjoy The read!
June J. McInerney

~~~~~~~~~~~~~~~~

THE

PRISONER'S PORTRAIT

~~~~~~~~~~~~~~~~

A Novel of Phoenixville During World War II

by

June J. McInerney

This is a work of fiction.
Names, characters, places, and incidents are mostly
figments of the author's imagination. Some are based
upon historical facts, real people, places, and businesses
which are used fictitiously and sometimes altered in the
best interests of telling a good story. Any resemblance to
actual persons, living or dead, business establishments,
organizations, events, and locales is, purely speculative
and often quite intentionally coincidental.

First Edition November 2015
Revised December 2015

ISBN-10: 1517759935
ISBN-13: 978-1517759933

Cover design by Doug Smith.

The portrait, *Luther at Wartburg* by F.W., is the property
of the University of Valley Forge. Permission has been
generously granted by UVF for use of the oil painting on
the cover of this novel.

Back cover picture of June and FrankieBernard
courtesy of the author.

B'Seti Pup Publishing
Phoenixville, PA
www.BSetiPupPublishing.com

Printed in the United States of America.

For all the prisoners of war
who honorably served...
on both sides.

*The only worst thing than being blind
is having sight but no vision.*
Helen Keller

Prologue

The tall, stocky woman in her mid-sixties drove her dusky grey-green Sebring convertible past the blue and bronze commemorative plaque erected a few years ago by the local historical society and turned right onto the university campus. She had put the black canvas top down to catch the weakening warm rays of an end-of-summer sun. Wisps of long, brown hair streaked with grey strayed from the thick chignon on the nape of her neck and fluttered in the cool early September breeze.

After spending most of the morning with her husband cleaning out the library that had once been her father's study, sorrowfully reminiscing as she sorted through the hundreds of books she and her family had collected throughout the years, she donated the majority of them to the local library as well as the Senior Citizens Center housed in the large grey stone building across from Firehouse Station 12. *Like my family, older people in this town are great readers,* she thought. *Our literary treasures will be put to good use there.*

Betty Fromüeller Guntherson had just retired from forty-five years of teaching Germanic and ancient Gaelic languages at Phoenixville High School. She and her husband, also a retired teacher, were permanently moving to Fort Lauderdale where they had just purchased a large two-bedroom condominium facing the ocean. The last two weeks had been busily spent packing up the large mansard roofed house on Gay Street that was once owned by her parents; where she had grown up with her two older siblings; and where she and Thor had raised their own four children.

With the books cleared off the library shelves – the older couple had overstuffed six large cardboard boxes with those they wanted to take with them – what was left of the rest of their belongings would be packed into the large Rent-a-Haul moving van now parked in their driveway. Settlement was scheduled for early tomorrow afternoon and Betty had precious little time left to run her few remaining errands. This was the last of them before heading home to finish the last minute packing and to start dinner before her husband returned from his last-day-in-town tennis match on the newly-furbished public courts on Mowere Road.

She parked the Sebring in the small lot in front of Harrup Hall, lifted the large oblong bubble-wrapped package form the back seat of the convertible, and walked proudly down the concrete path to the main entrance of the Storms Research Center.

She recalled the few times on Saturday mornings long ago when she and her brother and sister had walked this very same path as they accompanied their father to the Valley Forge General Hospital where he conducted Lutheran services for the German prisoners of war. She remembered that she and Max and Emily were afraid, but that their father had gently and compassionately allayed their fears.

"*Don't sie Angst, meine Lieben*," she remembered him saying soothingly as they walked to the small church alongside the stockade built behind the hospital buildings. "Don't you worry, my dears. You need not be afraid because the guards will protect you while I am preaching."

Betty looked beyond the large grey and white building that housed the university's research center and vast library. Instead of the stockade with its many rows of long red brick buildings surrounded by double rows of barbed-wire fencing, there were a large expanse of grass, a soccer field, a horseshoe pitch, and a small flower garden with a marble fountain. The modest chapel, she smiled, was still standing; its short steeple sporting a fresh coat of paint.

"I'm here to see the associate director," she whispered to the young student sitting behind the circulation desk. "Julia Patton? I called her earlier…"

"Down the hallway to the first door on the left," he explained, standing up. "Shall I help you with that?" indicating the package she was holding.

"No, thank you. I think we're fine."

"Mrs. Guntherson!" Julia exclaimed coming out of her office to greet her visitor. "We are so thrilled…that you called…that you're donating this to our university!" Her bright, brown eyes shone with excitement as she took the bubble-wrapped package from the older woman. She casually brushed back long, shiny brunette tresses away from her slender face and led the way through the open door. "Come in. Please. Have a seat."

Betty followed and sat on one of the molded plastic chairs in front of Julia's desk. She watched closely as the young woman carefully unwrapped the package and placed the oil painting on top of the small bookcase between floor-to-ceiling windows that looked out across an expanse of lawn. Julia stepped back to admire the detailed artistry and the colors still vivid after all these years.

Both women stared at the painting.

In it, a young man dressed in an early Sixteenth Century long red robe slouched against a large, leafy tree that shadowed what looked like the walls of a castle. A flurry of four white doves cavorted at his feet. He held a small book in front of him, but was glancing away from it, staring thoughtfully across the courtyard.

"Martin Luther at Wartburg Castle in 1521," Betty said. "I remember the afternoon my father brought it home. My mother hated that rustic, gold-tinted grooved wooden frame. It did not fit in with her taste and their décor, she had complained. It certainly wasn't something they would have purposely bought.

"But my father was adamant. He said, 'It was

made with such caring, um, patient hands...' I remember him smiling at his small joke. 'And it is part of this gift...to me. It shall stay here as is.'"

"And the artist...?" Julia asked.

"Apparently a young German prisoner of war held in captivity here...But my father would never reveal his name. Yet...See? His initials, F.W., are painted in brown in the lower right corner."

Julia squinted at the lettering and then carefully scrutinized the painting as her guest continued.

"The painting hung for the last sixty years or more over the mantle in my father's study," Betty explained. "He was, as you know, the Reverend Frederick Yohan Fromüeller, pastor of Bethany Evangelical Lutheran Church. The church is closed now.

"The small congregation merged with another parish from Spring City to form St. John's Lutheran Church...off South Whitehorse. The brownstone building with its brilliant crystal leaded windows – I'll never forget how the morning sun shimmered through the rose window over the altar – and its tall, arched red doors. It's long since been converted to office space...

"When my parents died, I and Thor – that's my husband, Thorstein – took over the house. That painting, mostly ignored, has stayed over the mantle in what is now, what was our library. Untouched, except for the occasional dusting. Until today.

"Well, I thought the university might like to have it," Betty mused. "Considering its history. Our new buyers don't want it and Thor and I won't be taking it with us." She chuckled. "It certainly doesn't fit in with our own condo décor."

"Please," Julia asked, "Do you know anything more about the painting?"

"Not much…" Betty said, "Except that the painter was quite young and very grateful to my father for often visiting him here. Every Saturday morning he would come to preach to and worship with the prisoners. Sorry, but I can't recall any more details…."

She stood up. "Well, I really must go now…" she said. "There is so much to do, now that my husband and I are moving…starting a new life…new beginnings…" She noticed Julia's wedding band. "Well, I am sure you know how it is."

The librarian smiled as Betty turned to leave.

"Are you sure," Julia asked, "that you really want us to have the young prisoner's work? That is...well...I mean, it was given to your father..."

"Yes, I am sure. It belongs here, where it was first painted. It has always been part of the university's history...not mine. This really is, after all, its home."

Julia watched as Mrs. Guntherson slowly walked out of the research center, and then turned back to the painting now safe and secure in her office.

"I wonder," she mused. "If there isn't more to the story..."

ONE

Early that cold, frosty February morning, Suzanne Elizabeth Kessler, bundled up in a long dark red, blue, and grey plaid woolen coat with a fraying beaver fur collar, briskly walked down the seven blocks from her parents' home on Second Avenue to the bus stop on the corner of Bridge and Main. She had promised her uncle she'd spend the rest of the week cataloguing and filing the last of the past three years' engine orders from both Boeing and the United States Army Air Corps before the government inspectors arrived on Monday to audit the books of Kessler and Gulden.

A last year's graduate of Phoenixville High School – class valedictorian, no less – she was a stickler for promptness and for keeping her promises. This was her first big chance since she started working as an assistant bookkeeper for Uncle Charles' company to prove, as her mother said, her "worth". Organizing and correctly filing the many complex orders would prove to him she was a valued employee and would, perhaps, help him and his partner, George Gulden, keep their nearly failing business afloat.

It was failing because, as the first few wintery months of 1945 began to wane into spring, the war was seemingly finally coming to a close, and engines for fighter jets, helicopters, and the large, lumbering B 17s, 19s, and 20s were no longer in such great demand. And commercial airlines across the country were not, for now or anytime in the foreseeable future while the war was still on, in need of propeller-driven engines. It seemed that when the conflagration in Europe was finally over, Kessler and Gulden might be out of business unless the massive machines and assembly lines were converted to peace-time manufacturing. Concentrating on her present tasks at hand, Suzanne would not, could not, and did not imagine what they might be making in the future instead of flight engines.

The bus was unusually late. It lagged behind a large convoy of slow moving open air lorries crammed with troops whom Suzanne first thought were United States soldiers. She couldn't see their faces clearly in the morning mist; just fragments of slightly soiled navy blue and dark khaki uniforms, a few splotches of blood showing through bandages. Some of the men jeered at her as they rode by; unfamiliar guttural sounds spouted from thin, parched lips. She shrugged and watched as the lorries rumbled passed her bus stop, then two more blocks down Bridge Street to make a left onto Route 113.

Some more of our wounded soldiers returning from the war on their way to Valley Forge General Hospital on Charleston Road, she surmised. She knew that army hospital trains that transported the maimed and sick from troop transport and hospital ships docking in Norfolk, New York, and Philadelphia made regular stops at the Penna railroad station, de-boarding their cargo onto ambulances and troop trucks for the last leg of the journey to the hospital. With the capacity to care for 3,000 wounded solders at a time, it was the largest military medical facility on the east coast and one of the largest employers in the borough, third only to the Steel Mill and the Phoenixville Iron Works. She waved as the lorries passed by, briefly catching the eye of a young soldier slumped in a corner.

Strange, she frowned. *His worsted wool brown*

*jacket...It doesn't look like a U.S. Army uniform...*She barely caught a glimpse of white lettering on his sleeve. *Maybe he's from a Special Forces unit.* Her father had once told her about the small cadres that made secret forays behind enemy lines, catching the Germans off guard and decimating their troops.

As her thoughts drifted into speculation, a mint green and white striped bus approached, edged its way to the curb, and stopped. Its folding doors opened onto the grey steel grated steps. She fumbled in her large square mottled handbag – cleverly made by her mother from a few scrapes of brocade upholstery fabric garnered from the trash bin of Quinn's Furniture store on Church Street – for her ten cent fare before getting on.

"You comin' or not?" the grim-faced bus driver scowled. She was surprised to see that he wasn't the youthful Smilin' Sam, the normal driver on the morning route to Pottstown, but a much older, grey-haired grouch. "Ain't got all day..." he grimaced.

"Yes, yes...I, um..." Suzanne stammered. "Just a sec...while I...Aha!" she said, finally finding a Liberty head mercury dime to put into the meter's slot when she climbed aboard.

"Well, get a move on then, young lady. Quit your dawdling. I got a schedule to keep, ya know..."

When she boarded, she asked, "What happened to Sam?"

"Don't know. Don't care. Probably off to war, I suspect...They're taking everyone these days...'cept a course, us old wiry ones..."

Suzanne wasn't sure if the new scowl that accompanied what she thought was a chuckle might have been a grin. She was the sort of girl who always tried to see the best in people, even if they were grouchy old bus drivers.

"Well, I just thought, if there was any way of finding out..." Despite his ignoring her most of the time, Suzanne, in the past nine months making her daily morning commute to Pottstown, had grown quite found of Sam, laughing at his corny jokes and grimacing at his off-key – and often off-color – renditions of the latest popular songs as he sang along with the blaring radio perched on the dashboard. *If he has gone off to war...Well, I would want to know...if nothing else...but to...*

"Take your seat, miss. Ain't got time for chitty-chattin'," the aging bus driver growled again, interrupting her thoughts. He pulled the large, steel lever to close the doors and edged the bus, sans jokes and music, back into the sparse Bridge Street traffic. Suzanne barely nodded to the ten or so other riders and settled into a window seat.

She gazed out, watching the buildings and houses of her hometown turn into barren countryside as the bus travelled north on Black Horse Road, passed the State Geriatric Center, to connect with the busy thoroughfare that led into Pottstown. Her thoughts idled back to the strangely dressed soldiers in the lorries. Their fuzzy images began to coalesce in her mind.

She sat up straight, suddenly realizing what she had seen. The large white lettering on their sleeves and back: PW. *Prisoners of war. The soldiers...the men in those trucks,* she nearly said out loud, glancing furtively at the other passengers. *They weren't our soldiers at all. They are German soldiers. Prisoners of war! Here in Phoenixville!?!* Just like *The Daily Republican* had reported last month that they would come...*Oh, good God...*

Suzanne was miffed that she had arrived much

later at work then she wanted. She prided herself on her to-the-second punctuality and her neat-as-a-pin, to-the-letter organizational skills. They were, Uncle Charles had said more often then not, the main reasons he had hired her – despite the fact she was his favorite niece. She had barely hung her hat and purse on the wooden hat rack in the corner near her desk in the small office just off the reception area and settled in to continue sorting the filled orders by year, month, and ordering company, when one of the newly-hired shipping clerks casually strolled in to place the invoices of his latest deliveries on her desk.

"Hello, Susie!" he smiled as she looked up from her tasks. She hated the diminutive form of her name and sniffed a curt "Hello!" back at him – hoping he'd get the message – and returned to her sorting and filing.

What was his name?

She had been briefly introduced to him when he started the job a week or so ago, but had quickly forgotten. Suzanne was great with faces; not so good with names. *It started with a "J". Jack? Jacob? Joe? Does it really matter? Not really.*

All she knew from the office rumor mill was that

he was recently discharged from the United States Army Air Corps. He had been a gunner in a ball turret, she was told, assigned to a "bubble" in the belly of a B17 Flying Fortress because of his slight height and weight. One of the most dangerous assignments in the war, she knew. He had flown, she was told, more than thirty missions, was shot down and miraculously had survived. A rarity, "they" said, noting that he was, also, in fact, a twice decorated hero.

But Susan was less impressed with his valiant heroism than with his demeanor, despite his rudeness in not acknowledging her preferred given name clearly displayed on the plaque on her desk. While Jack/John/Joe/Jacob was shorter than most men she knew, he was quite handsome and muscularly built; her father would say like an inverted concrete pyramid: He was broad in the shoulders, with his solid chest tapering to a slender, compact waist. The sort of man, she unconsciously smiled inwardly, that would be nicely compatible with her own lithe, small, just a tad over five foot frame.

"I saw that," he said.

"What?"

"I saw that smile, Susie! Was it, perhaps, for me?"

"Er…No. Maybe…No!"

"Susie Kessler. Right?"

"No, I am Suzanne Kessler," she snapped, exaggerating her first name, pointing to the plaque. "See?!" She stuffed yet another completed order into the file folder marked "1944". "*Suzanne* Kessler," she repeated. "And you are…?

"John…John Voight the Second. Johnny for short. Whoops, pardon the pun," he smiled again, exaggeratingly stretching up to his full height of five-foot-four and smartly saluting. "At your service. Ma'am!"

Suzanne bristled, then softened, and then chuckled at his courtesy. She mocked his gesture, saluting smartly back. Not only was she instantly attracted to his physical build, she had to admit that she also somehow liked his easy-going élan and sense of humor.

"I heard you were in the Blitz…flew over Germany?"

"Many times before…and since then…before I

was finally, um, disabled... and," he laughed, "able to come home." He rubbed his left shoulder absentmindedly, as if in some nascent pain. "I bombed a lot of those Nazis all to hell...before they..." he mumbled. "Oh, sorry. Pardon my language. But...um, I'd rather not think about it now...talk about it...any more. You know."

"Sorry...but..."

"It's okay, Susie," he wanly grinned. "Lots of people ask...But, as I said, I'd rather not talk about it...Let's talk about you."

The Reverend Frederick Yohan Fromüeller, the pastor of the small Bethany Evangelical Lutheran Church on Morgan Street, knew that approximately 250 Germany prisoners of war were to arrive at the Valley Forge General Hospital from a holding camp in eastern Michigan in early February. A member of the Lutheran Commission on Prisoners of War, he had received a letter two months ago explaining that they were being culled from the 511 or so PW camps across the country and transported by train to the Valley Forge General Hospital complex.

Members of the German *Medical Korps* in some

capacity or other, the prisoners were to help alleviate the shortage of personnel required to care for the patients, United States armed forces members wounded in the war. The 3,000 bed hospital, built in 1942 and the only military one in the country named for a place, was filled to capacity and a large number of the 1,200-member staff had been re-assigned overseas. Those remaining were overworked, badly in need of assistance.

In the letter the commission requested that since he spoke fluent German as well as English he was to ensure that Lutheran prisoners were offered the "...solace of weekly worship services and adequate preaching." They also were to be made to feel welcomed in and by "...your small church community in Phoenixville".

After five years serving their congregation, the middle-aged, big, burly yet gentle and affable Reverend Fromüeller, affectingly dubbed "Pastor Freddy", had come to know its members quite well. Providing worship services for the prisoners at VFGH was one thing. Welcoming them into their midst was quite another. Besides, he had heard that most of the other camps forbade prisoners from leaving the grounds unless they were out on work detail. And only then under heavy guard. He knew that his constituents, as well as other residents of the sleepy town, neatly nestled into the small hills of northern Chester County, would be up in arms at the prospect of "the enemy", albeit prisoners, being in their midst.

He had confided the information to Abram Kessler, one of the elders of the church who worked as an engineer at the hospital. But the reverend decided it best not to tell anyone else. Not even his beloved spouse. Besides, she had enough on her plate being the busy, popular wife of a rector, taking care of their three rambunctious toddlers, and refurbishing their large 100-year old house on Gay Street.

Two

The arrival of the prisoners at the Valley Forge General Hospital was the main topic of conversation over dinner that night. Suzanne's father had folded *The Daily Republican* to the long article on the second page and passed it around the table. He acted as surprised as his family was when they read the news, refraining from telling them that Pastor Freddy had told him about it weeks ago, but had sworn him to secrecy. The reverend was concerned that any prior overt knowledge would frighten the congregation; not that Abram would even think of telling anyone. Not even his wife and children. Especially not the children.

"So," Suzanne sighed as she pushed small bits of stringy corned beef and boiled cabbage around her plate. She was tired of the poor, tasteless quality – and small quantity – of rationed meat and the acrid taste of less than fresh vegetables. Briefly glancing at the article, she sighed, and then handed it to her younger sister. "That's who they really were...the ones I saw this morning."

"Who, dear?" her mother asked, rising to fetch a newly warmed homemade apple cobbler from the kitchen.

"They were packed like sardines in the backs of huge lorries that passed by while I was waiting for the bus. I thought at first they were our American soldiers. But, then, their uniforms were strange...not like any I recognized. Then I thought they wouldn't be looking so...well...rag tag."

"Rag tag?" her father asked, spooning a bit of his wife's "famous" cobbler onto his plate. "That's an odd expression for you to use, Suzanne..."

"They looked a bit...oh, I don't know...rough, dirty. Some even seemed to leer at me. Not something our boys would do, would they? And then I realized...But I was occupied with being late for work and anxious for the bus to come. So I didn't think about it anymore...and didn't really care...I hadn't noticed at first...but then until...I later realized..."

"Until...? You realized?" her mother asked.

"They had...large white letters. PW. Sewn on their clothes. And then John, the new shipping clerk at work said that, yes, it was true. They were prisoners." Suzanne frowned in thought.

"Yes," Abram Kessler said. "According to the article, not only are most of the prisoners German, but they are doctors, medics, and orderlies culled from PW camps in southwestern United States to assist our sparse staff at the hospital with caring for our American wounded."

He paused, and then smiled. "So, you met young Johnny Voight today, huh?

"Poppa, do you know who he is?"

"Yes, I do. I am surprised you do not remember him. The Voights are members of our church."

"No, Poppa...I don't remember." Suzanne thought back to their conversation that morning. "Although, his name did sound slightly familiar...He's much older than I am...Isn't he?"

"That's right, dear," her mother chimed in. "Almost six years...Now," she smiled, trying to change the subject, "eat your cobbler."

"Yes, Momma..." Her head down, Suzanne swished a small mount of baked apple around the bowl with a teaspoon for a few minutes, musing about the young clerk back from the war who teasingly called her "Susie". When she finally looked up, she turned toward her father. "Tell me more about him, Poppa. All I heard were rumors about him at work. Was he really a ball turret gunner? He didn't talk much about the war...Didn't seem to want to..."

"Understandable," Abram Kessler said, sipping his chicory flavored coffee. "Our boys went...are going through a lot over there. Talking about it dredges up painful memories. More painful than we could ever fathom or even understand. Best not to ask him directly..."

Suzanne smiled wanly at her father's compassionate and sage words. He was, as a matter of fact, the wisest person she knew. She strived to be like him, hoping that someday someone would say the same thing about her.

"His father is the Borough's Parks and Recreation Director," Abram continued, ignoring his wife's stern looks, begging him not to talk any more about the war at the dinner table. "Bad for the indigestion," she constantly chided. But her husband adamantly continued. "He maintains the public tennis courts on Jones Street. Wasn't John...Johnny in school with you?"..."

When she realized why John's last name sounded vaguely familiar, she quizzically smiled.

"I guess. I know his father. Everyone in town knows 'Mr. Racket' but I really don't remember his son. As Momma says, he was at least five, six years ahead of me...But you know all about him, don't you, Poppa?" she asked, knowing full well that as an elder of the small church on Morgan Street, he made it a point to know as much as he could about each and every one of his fellow parishioners whom he considered family. Besides working as an engineer at the Valley Forge General Hospital, he made it his life's avocation to know about – and help – his fellow church members as well as his employees as best he could.

She smiled shyly at him, pushing the half-eaten bowl of cobbler away. "Please, Poppa...Tell me..."

"Well, Johnny Voight is just a few weeks out of the service..." Abram stated. "Received a medical discharge with honors."

"What happened to him?"

"His father told me that Johnny caught some shrapnel in the shoulder when his plane was strafed by a German Luftwaffe Messerschmitt over Lille,

France. They had just crossed the English Channel on their way to bomb munitions factories in Stuttgart," Suzanne's father explained as he finished dessert. "The plane, a B17 Flying Fortress named the 'Betty Boop', I think, was forced to turn around and land in a field in northern France...near the coast. The farmer, the owner of the field, commandeered a small flotilla of fishermen to sail the rest of the crew back to England..."

"And Johnny...er, John?" Suzanne asked. She was not found of diminutive nicknames, neither for himself nor for others. In that vein, she thought of the heroic ball turret gunner, now newly-hired shipping clerk, as "John", not "Johnny".

"Johnny...Yes. John," Abram smiled at his older daughter's prim correctness. "Well, the farmer and his wife kept him hidden in the attic for a while, furtively trying to nurse his wounds. But as the Germans advanced, they decided it would be best to take him hidden under a layer of straw in the back of their wagon to an American army field medical unit just across the Belgian border. After some make-shift patching up, he was shipped back home on a hospital troop ship – his chest and arm heavily swathed in bandages – along with other wounded army personnel. He spent some time – a few months, actually – recuperating at VFGH. But it was apparent that with his injuries, he could no longer handle a turret machine gun. So, he was discharged."

"How did he get to work for Kessler and Gulden?"

"Well, after services one Sunday, Mr. Voight told me the story and asked if I knew of a job for his son..."

"So, you got him the job..."

"Yep, I did. I, um, know your uncle. Remember?" He laughed at his joke. Suzanne smiled wryly, joining him in his dry mirth. Charles Kessler, her uncle, was, of course her father's older brother. "Charlie tries to help all returning servicemen who are willing to work. A good man, Johnny is. Young, but experienced. I understand he loves to keep inventory..."

Abram smiled at his oldest child, now a mature young woman with sparkling dusty-grey-blue eyes, a lithe, short, but very attractive, boyishly feminine figure. A thick shock of shiny ebon hair curled over her shoulders and down her back. *With her brilliantly astute mind, musical and culinary talents*, he thought, *any man...maybe young Johnny...John Voight...would be lucky—too lucky – to have her as his wife*. He chuckled again.

"You might want to cultivate his, um, friendship..." he said. "Bet you couldn't find a finer man around to...well, marry. You know....isn't it time you started thinking..."

"Abram!" Katerina Kessler interrupted, chiding her husband. "Stop teasing the girl. Look, she's blushing..."

"All I was saying that now that she is...."

"Enough, Abram! You've been nagging at her ever since her eighteenth birthday. Our Suzanne will make up her own mind when she is ready..."

"Momma..." Suzanne managed to swallow her embarrassment and asked, "What if I am not ready? Yet?"

"Hah!" Ruth Ann, Suzanne's little sister squealed, looking up from the paper. She had read the PW article twice, carefully underlining each word with her fingers as she studied it. "That will be the day when Miss Fuzzy Pants is ready to have a *boyfriend*!" She elongated "boy", savoring the "o" sound and smirked.

Suzanne sat quietly, feeling more blood flushing her cheeks and forehead. Perspiration beaded on her upper lip. She knew better than to verbally spar with her quick-witted sibling, who always won their arguments and nearly always got her way.

Unlike herself, Ruth Ann was spoiled; her every whim was indulged by their parents. It was a sharp bone of contention between the two sisters; a bone that Suzanne often gnawed upon, but refrained from complaining about in order to keep peace in their small family.

Instead of speaking up, she retreated into her mind, dwelling on how sweet her new thoughts felt: the improbable prospect of perhaps, as her father suggested, getting to know John Voight better and, dare she even consider it? Maybe, just maybe. Someday. Eventually. Marrying him. She was that – uncharacteristically – smitten. *Is it really true,* she wondered, *about "love at first sight"?*

Ruth Ann watched her sister blush and clam up. *Just like her to not say anything. Afraid of provoking me, she is,* she thought with glee. She chuckled, smirked again, and said to no one in particular, "I knew it! Never, every ready! Never will be."

Suzanne clenched her month shut and made a fist in her lap under the table. *Never will be...will never be true,* she glowered inwardly. *Just you wait and see, little sister. Just you wait and see.*

Ruth Ann squinted at her older sibling as if she could read Suzanne's mind, smiled at her parents sweetly, and then slid the newspaper over to her father.

"Tell us more about the prisoners, Poppa dear," she crooned in what Suzanne had come to recognize as Ruth Ann's fake sickly-sweet cajoling voice used whenever she wanted something. Her parents fell for it every time. "I do so want to know..."

THREE

Franz, slouched in one corner of the drab olive U.S. Army lorry crowded with thirty other captured members of various German medical units, rubbed his arms against the chilly morning air. Even though made of wool, his new, U.S. Army issued pseudo-khaki brown prisoner of war jacket was not sufficient enough to keep him warm. He stuffed his hands under his armpits and tucked his chin into the wide collar trying to avoid the wind.

A solitary young man with, he was quickly learning, quite different political views and ideas of decorum than most of his fellow travelers, he did not participate in the jeering and leering at the young woman on the concrete sidewalk who watched as they passed by. He was ashamed of their behavior.

We are supposed to be professionals – doctors, medics...They are acting like common buffoons.

He frowned at their cocky, disrespectful demeanor. Unacceptable, even though they were now in the hands and country of their enemy.

Their enemy, he thought to himself. *I wanted*

nothing to do with this war. Nothing! I want, more than anything else, to be back with my mother on our small farm just outside Eisenach. My studies, he moaned, *I want to continue my medical studies at Efburt University…to be able to draw, to paint…to be free once again…Yes! Dare I think, hope? To…pray?* Yet, here he was, with large white PW letters sewn haphazardly on the back of his jacket, on his sleeves, and down his pant legs.

Branded, like a common pig. I am not like them, he thought. *Louts, cads, cruel murderers. Even if some of them are doctors. I was once like that girl…young, innocent. Until the* Deutches Jungvolk *sucked me in.*

Even with his head lowered onto his chest, he was able to catch the girl's eye. *Kind, a sparkling dusty-grey shade of blue,* he had noticed. *Soft, gentle.* He smiled shyly and thought he saw her smile back.

Perhaps the movement of her hand to open her purse was a wave?

He continued to stare at her, trying to smile with his eyes, until the lorry reached the corner of Route 113 and turned left and she had disappeared from his sight.

I will never forget those eyes. So much like

Greta's. Franz choked back a sob, remembering his childhood sweetheart and their last goodbyes before he was marched off to join an infantry unit as a medic.

The young American lady looked so much like her, Franz sighed, whispering to himself. *Someday, I will be free. I will go home. I will find my Greta and once again gaze into those eyes...*

Four

It was early on his sixteenth birthday when the two officers knocked heavily on the slatted wooden door of their small farmhouse. The sun had just barely risen and Franz was still drifting in the warm twilight between barely waking and wanting to stay asleep. Dreaming of exploring more of the castle fortress that afternoon, he thought he had heard the rumble of a motor car in the distance. But since motorcars were not allowed across the ancient moat, he continued with his adventure, standing on the bench built around the circumference of the large oak tree that shaded much of the courtyard, reaching up to catch a low bough to hoist himself up into a crook between two of its branches. It was his favorite hiding place; waking or sleeping.

The pounding continued, growing louder with each hammering blow. Finally, he heard the creak of the door as it slowly opened and the hollow stomping of boots on the stone floor. One of the men grumbled a despondent whisper as they forced their way in.

"Franz! *Libchen*!" his mother yelled up the wide ladder that led to his sleeping loft. "You must get up. Now!" Her voice sounded frantic, almost panicky. High pitched. Not like her usual, calm, stoic, soothing low alto.

"I am coming, *Mutter*," he called down, peering over the edge of the loft. Despite the early morning, his mother had promise to let him sleep in that day, forgoing his chores. He watched as the men, dressed in brown shirted uniforms and black belts with leather straps across their left shoulders, peered around the great room, taking in details: the beginnings of breakfast scattered upon the large, hand-hewn table nicked and worn by generations of use; the breakfront crammed with his mother's treasured Dresden china; the faint flicker of the day's just lit first fire; the cast-iron pot of nut-flavored oatmeal steaming over it; and on it the small skillet with slabs of bacon just beginning to fry; and the many oil paintings – some framed, most of them not – haphazardly hung on the walls. The burlier of the German soldiers marched across the room and poked at his mother's small bed by the hearth. He rummaged through the bedclothes and jabbed a riding crop through her meager personal belongings.

"Are you hiding anything, anybody else besides your son?" the Gestapo lieutenant asked. His mother shook her head, afraid to speak directly to him who, with his assistant lackey, had rudely invaded her home. "Well, Frau Weberhardt?!" he demanded, watching her. "What else...Whom else are you hiding?"

"Nobody," his mother whispered. Franz had never seen nor heard her be so afraid. Or so cowed.

"*Person jüdischer?* A Jew, perhaps? A young girl? About seventeen?"

"*Nein. Nein*! No. I swear."

"We shall soon see..." he said, slapping the crop against the side of his boot. As he nodded to a young officer to continue the search, a hastily dressed and very angry Franz shimmied down the ladder and wedged his tall, lithe, muscular frame between the lieutenant and his mother.

"Leave her alone!" he shouted as the lackey began to knock on walls and open cupboard doors, throwing, strewing, and breaking household items upon the floor. "And leave our stuff alone! It is me you've come for, isn't it?"

"Ach, *Ja!* The young lad. Yes. It is you we wish to see. You've avoided joining the Hitler Youth for a long time, now." He waved dismissively to his assistant to discontinue the search. "You are now sixteen...too old to childishly cling to your mother's apron strings and shirk your duties to the Fatherland. You must now join the *Deutches Jungvolk*. Farm chores and illnesses are not excuses. Your first priority now is to our Fuehrer. *Uber alles!*"

"I do not wish to...serve...him," Franz said unabashedly. "I have had other, more important...better things to do than march around like an idiot and lie about my friends." He thought of his new friend, Greta, whose family had recently moved to the small farm he had to walk past on his way to the castle.

Instantly smitten two weeks ago by the dark-haired, grey-blue eyed lass standing by the hedgerow watching two goshawks lazily circling overhead, he immediately asked her to join him in his secret spot where they soon began trading childhood secrets that would ultimately, and furtively, turn into adult intrigues and eventual nightmares.

"Oh, you do, do you?" The brown-shirted lieutenant gripped Franz's ear lobe and started to twist it. "I've a good mind to arrest you now for treason and insubordination. But, as I am in a good mood today...I will not. Even if you are an insolent brat."

"Then you will leave," Franz asserted himself, trying very hard not to wince with the pinching pain.

"Leave him be!" Frau Weberhardt shouted, grabbing the officer's shoulder. "You are hurting him!"

"Yes, I will leave," he said, shrugging off Franz's mother and, giving it another sharp twist, let go of Franz's ear. "But with a warning. You will report tomorrow morning to the civic center. You will be there promptly at nine o'clock or I will come back tomorrow afternoon and personally escort you in chains. And destroy your cozy little country home in the process. Do you understand? You will join the Young Folk. You will serve! Heil Hitler!"

Rubbing his swelling ear that was starting to turn beet red, Franz stood defiantly by his mother. "Yes, sir!" he mocked. "But not by choice."

Later that afternoon, after assiduously doing his

chores, Franz packed a small knapsack with a wedge of Stilton cheese, four roasted sausages, a large half-loaf of freshly baked pumpernickel, and two bottles of his mother's homemade apple cider. He ran across the flower-strewn fields to fetch Greta. They were going to explore together more of the area around the castle. He was also excited to tell her the story of one of his childhood heroes: Martin Luther and his sojourn in the fort of Wartburg after being excommunicated in 1521 by Pope Leo X. But Franz promised himself that he would not tell his new confident that the Gestapo had called upon him right after sunrise and that he had to join the *Hitlerjugend.*

Greta, a year older than the lithe young lad, while mildly interested in the local history, he would learn, was anxious to talk of more pressing, current matters and the dire plans her family was being forced to make.

Five

"Hey, *Hitlerjugend!*" an unkempt, rough-looking staff sergeant yelled to him from the other side of the lorry. Franz looked up at Otto Kempf, one of the most vociferous, violent, and volatile members of the group who had continually boasted on the train ride from Michigan that he had served as a medic with Rommel's *Afrika Korps* before his unit was captured by American forces just outside Tunisia. "But not without a fight – from me!" Otto had often decried until one of the U.S. Army Military Police officers ordered him to "stand down and be silent". Franz sneered in disgust at his demeanor, as well as his appearance. Staff Sergeant Otto or Herr Kempf, as he demanded to be called – "As befitting my station as a medical *Oberfeldwebel!*" – swiped his hand over his mouth, smearing the mucus that leaked from his bulbous red nose and dribbled down his chin onto his stained, blood-encrusted jacket.

It sickened Franz to look at him. German doctors and their assistants, he had learned during his first year of medical studies, are supposed to be neat and tidy, not gruff and dirty. Franz looked at the other men seated in the lorry with him. All except Otto were dressed in the new pristine PW uniforms issued to them when they first arrived at Fort Custer from the various camps from which were culled. All, except Otto, were only slightly soiled from their long three-day journey by bus, train, and truck across the American countryside. His eyes drifted back to Otto. *All, except for slovenly Kempf. Common lout. He's a disgrace to our profession. And to our country.*

"What were you gaping at? Ogling that chicky-chick back there, huh?!" Otto snickered. "*Verdammt es, man!* You're too young to be thinking lewd thoughts about American girls…Besides…"

"Shut up, Otto," Franz gritted between his teeth, wishing he could wipe the snide grin, as well as the snot, from the older man's face. He reminded Franz of the rude Gestapo lieutenant who had first visited his farm home so long ago, conscripting him into the Hitler Youth movement. "You don't know what I am thinking!"

"Nor do I want to," Otto snorted, again wiping his mouth with the back of his sleeve. "But, I surmise. Hah! I would love to see the nude painting you do of her when you once again get paints and brushes back into your hands. If these American pigs even let you have them. Something for all of us to enjoy while being held captive by the Jew-lovers, eh?" It was painfully obvious to Franz, as well as the other German prisoners, that Herr Kempf, like many of them, was a pro-Nazi, with total, blinding allegiance to Hitler and his hatred for anything non-Aryan.

"*Oh Gott's Sake*, Otto!" the sub-lieutenant sitting next to Franz shouted. "He's just a young man who has already seen and done far too much for his tender years. Leave him alone...to his own thoughts. He will paint what he wants, when he wants. When, and if, he is allowed to...where we're going..."

"Shuddup, back there, you dirty Krauts!" Lieutenant Quisling called back from the cab of the lorry. "This ain't no sightseeing tour!" The Army Military Policeman raised his Colt .45 pistol and pointed it through the open window separating the lorry's cab from the back, threatening to shoot.

Although he had strict orders, governed by what he thought were the archaic Geneva Conventions of 1929, to make sure the Nazi prisoners were humanely treated and safely transported to their interment stockade at the Valley Forge General Hospital, Eric Quisling would have given anything to have an excuse to kill one, some, even all of his PW charges. *Conventions be damned!*

Otto turned to Quisling, mouthed a German obscenity, and then spat a large spume of phlegm at the open window. Some of the other prisoners laughed and jeered along with Otto at their captor, knowing full well he was not allowed to shot them, even if justly provoked.

"I said, shut the fuck up!! *Verschlossen warden!*" Quisling shouted again, twisting around in the passenger seat to stick his arm through the window. "*Verstehen?*" He waved the pistol back and forth, aiming in turn at each one of the prisoners. "Okay! Who wants it?" he asked. Otto laughed out loud, jeering more German obscenities at Quisling. "Keep it up, boys, and I will shoot. I'd rather deliver a full load of dead prisoners to the hospital for burial than half a lorry of live Nazi Krauts who we gotta feed and keep alive. Which will it be?"

Otto smirked again and then suddenly stopped laughing and swearing. Signaling the rest of the men to be quiet, he sullenly looked away from Quisling and curled up into a large furry bear-like ball against one wooden-slatted wall of the lorry. Quisling smiled a discourteous *Vielen Dank* – Thank you – and turned back in his seat. He carefully, almost lovingly cradled his gun in his lap for the rest of their short journey.

It took a good twenty minutes for the seven lorries to travel in the freezing cold from the train station to the Valley Forge hospital complex. A light snow had started to fall earlier that morning, now reducing visibility to a minimum. Large portions of the route were iced over. The Army MP drivers slowed the vehicles to a crawl to avoid skidding on the black rime. By the time they had reached their destination, despite being somewhat sheltered by the canvas side flaps from the biting wind and heavy snow, Franz and the other prisoners were shivering.

"This is nothing like the cozy, plush passenger cars we rode in from the camp at Fort Custer in Michigan," Franz whispered into his hands, hoping his breath would keep them warm. He had made it a point to learn all the places he had been since arriving at what he had learned from the guards was "stateside". "Imagine!" he exclaimed, remembering the warmth. "Such luxury, even in wartime."

The sub-lieutenant next to him smiled, also remembering the irony of being treated like proper gentlemen, courteously served hot coffee, sandwiches, and donuts by polite black stewards clad in the crisp, white starched jacketed uniforms of the Pennsylvania Railroad.

"I think our captors are so afraid of mistreating us," he said, "lest word gets back to the Fatherland and there is retaliation against the American soldiers being held in our own country...that they are certainly overdoing it."

Franz smiled warily, despite his chills. He had taught himself long ago to distrust all German officers, even if they were, like himself, prisoners of war. "Maybe...you are right. Sir? *Herr Doktor?*"

"A doctor? Yes. Orthopedics. A bone-setter...And you?"

Franz was unwilling to open up to a superior officer. *Yet,* he thought, *A kindly face...perhaps he is not like the others.* "I finished my first year of medical studies at Efburt University," he coughed against the growing tightness in his chest.

"But you were a member of the Hitler Youth Movement?"

"Some of us were allowed to study, provided we went to the morning meetings," he said crisply, not wishing to reveal more than he thought others should know. "But when I turned eighteen, I was conscripted into the Army. I wanted...want to be an eye surgeon...but my studies were interrupted. I was assigned as a medic to a unit fighting its way up southern Italy to Rome..."

"Where you were captured?"

"Yes. In battle. Near the Volturna River." Franz shivered again, this time not from the cold, but from the freshly carved memories of being force-marched, then driven behind enemy lines to Naples where he was crammed along with hundreds of other German prisoners of war into a holding pen for three days and then onto the steel decks of an empty U.S. Maritime Marine troop ship for transport across the Atlantic Ocean. "Frightening...not knowing where I, we were going. Or why...except that we were in the hands of the enemy we were told were brutal murderers."

"Turns out they are not," the doctor said. "Except, perhaps, for that Quisling....And a few American fortune...souvenir hunters that stole our belongings and ripped the buttons and medals off our uniforms...Not to mention our *soldbuches* that contained all of our personal and military information. I see you still have yours," indicating the small leather pouch firmly attached to Franz's belt.

"Yes...But he..." Franz looked up at the MP sitting shotgun. "Certainly he is...a regular megalomaniac. Like Hit..." Franz stopped before uttering the Fuehrer's name, assuming that the sub-lieutenant was, like Otto, probably also a harden National Socialist. Fearing some sort of brutal reprisal he had heard about while in other camps, he refused to say anything more. But he couldn't help thinking it.

Like a few others who were compelled at tender ages to join the *Deutches Jungvolk* and march daily for hours in hot, scratchy uniforms shouting "*Heil, Mein Fuehrer!*" over and over until his throat was red raw, he hated Adolph Hitler's ideas, ideals, and ambitions. He hated being ripped from his mother and their beloved bucolic farm life, coerced to attend rallies and youth meetings. He despised being forced to give up his medical studies and his painting to serve in a war that, to him, had no rhyme or reason. All he ever wanted was to be home to live, draw, and study in peace...and to be with Greta.

"Not to worry, son. Unlike our friend, Otto, over there, I believe I share...sympathize with your feelings..." The doctor looked at the large manila tag tied to a button on Franz's tunic. "Weberhardt, huh? Where are you from? In Germany, I mean..."

Still not trusting the doctor in the crisp, barely soiled uniform, Franz paused for a few moments. Then, when he had smiled at him, Franz said, "Eisenach. A small farm..."

"*Ah, ja*. North of Berlin. Wartburg Castle is there, is it not?"

"Yes," Franz grinned. "You know of it?"

"Every good..." he paused and cleared his throat, "Lutheran knows about it...It's our history. Where Martin Luther hid out in 1521 to 1522 from Leo X when he was excommunicated after refusing to recant his ninety-five theses..."

"Yes," Franz said crisply, cutting he doctor off. "I

am well aware of the story. But actually, he was held captive..." Luther was, to him, if not for being excommunicated, what he thought a real saint should be. He refused to have the Reformer's name and life's achievements bantered about like so much common gossip in the back of a dirty lorry.

He slunk back into his thin jacket, remembering how he told Greta that Luther had railed against the Catholic Church's practice, among others, of indulgences and his belief in redemption totally based upon faith.

She had looked at him in total disbelief.

"That matters not to me," she had said, sitting on the bench in the courtyard, brushing dry oak leaves from her fraying green dirndl. "What a Christian does or believes...Franz...I must tell you...I am...*ein Jüdisches Mädchen*. A Jew..."

"Yes!" the doctor exclaimed, oblivious to Franz's withdrawal, wishing to expound his own knowledge to this young, reticent young lad. "His *September Testament*, a translation of the new one from Greek to German was accomplished in just under ten weeks!"

"I know that," Franz said. "As you said, every

good Lutheran knows that. Common knowledge. It solidified the Reformation."

"Sorry...I just thought we had something in common. Unlike the others." He, too, slunk back on the lorry bench and stared out into the rapidly falling snow.

Franz was startled, and a bit remorseful. They were forbidden in the Fatherland to admit their religious tendencies, let alone think or even discuss amongst themselves their faith and beliefs. And, yet, here was a fellow German – an officer, even – one of those he had vowed not to trust – who had openly talked about Luther.

He thought back to his mother who prayed secretly every morning and night, kneeling reverently at the small, plain wooden altar he had built for her in one of their barn stalls. When just a mere child sitting on her lap, he had learned to recite the *Vater Unser*, sing a few hymns, and eclipse the true meaning of his own budding abiding faith.

When he was old enough to venture out on his own, he often walked the two miles or so to Wartburg Castle to roam the courtyard where Luther had walked and sat praying as he contemplated his own life, the profound effects he was having on the Church, and his new-found conviction of salvation by faith alone. Franz empathized with the loneliness the reformer must have felt being isolated from his friends and family.

Much like he now felt as a prisoner of war.

"Yes…I, um, know," he shyly offered, hoping the doctor would sense his contriteness. "Luther would never have condoned this…war. Would he have? He was after all, a monk. A man of peace…"

"No, Franz Weberhardt. I don't think he would have. Nor should we, *ja*?" The doctor paused and looked up. "Looks like we've finally arrived. Quite a large complex…" Franz shied away as the officer tried to pat his shoulder. "Hang in there, son," he said confidently.

"We'll get through this. Soon the war will be over. And we'll be home once again."

Six

The guardhouse of the Valley Forge General Hospital was a short, squat square one-story building. Its wooden frame had been slathered with tar paper and then covered with pine shingles painted a deep cobalt blue. Five large clerestory windows faced the entrance to the hospital complex on Charlestown Road. Another large window looked out onto the single-lane road that led from the entrance to the side of the administration building and beyond to the web of macadam roads and overhead corridors that crisscrossed the 182-acre campus connecting most of the 100-plus buildings. Two large red and white striped sawhorses stretched across the lane, blocking access to all but pedestrian traffic.

The first of the seven-lorry convoy pulled up to the window facing the lane. After a few minutes of waiting, Sergeant Augustus Cooper jumped out of the driver's seat of the first truck and rapped upon the glass of the side window.

"Anyone home?!" he hollered, failing to notice

the Military Police guard stepping out from the back of the building.

"Yo! What's up?!?" the guard called, zipping up his trousers. "Can't anyone take a leak in privacy around here without being rudely interrupted?" He swung the automatic rifle slung over his shoulder into his hands and pointed it at Cooper. "Name, rank, and serial number!"

"I, um...Well, as you can see," the sergeant gestured toward the seven lorries queued in line from the guardhouse to the edge of Charlestown Road. "I have a convoy of German prisoners of war..."

The guard surveyed the men dressed in PW uniforms crammed in the back of the trucks, then clicked off the safety of his rifle and cocked the hammer. "How do I know this is not an invasion of some kind? You Nazis are a cagey bunch!" he barked,

"Drop your weapon, corporal," Lieutenant Quisling shouted as he jumped down from the third lorry and aimed his pistol over the lorry's hood straight at the guard. "I am not a Nazi, but those guys in the trucks are...But we come in peace...so sayeth the Lord. As my buddy here said!" he yelled, briefly pointing his pistol barrel at Cooper. "We are Military Police delivering a contingent of two hundred and fifty German prisoners to this facility. But, so help me God, if you don't calm down and let us through to deposit our cowardly cargo, I will...Shoot. You. Dead. Got that? Soldier?"

The guard looked warily at Quisling, then at Cooper, and then scanned the seven lorries each packed with thirty-five Germans. He looked back at Quisling.

"Yes, Sir! But...you were not expected today. Where are your...the papers? Show me your papers! SIR!" he shouted, still aiming his rifle at Cooper's chest.

"Hold your fire. I'll get them," Sergeant Cooper whispered, edging his way back to the first lorry. He reached into the passenger window and opened the glove box where he kept the State Department's orders and transport papers for the delivery of the prisoners. "Here they are. Co-signed by an Adjutant General and Colonel Henry Beakers, the hospital post Commanding Officer and Chief Medical Officer himself!" he blustered proudly.

While still not completely satisfied that

everything was, as he put it, "according to Hoyle", the guard reluctantly handed the papers back, then sloppily saluted both Cooper and Quisling. He took his time moving the crossing gates aside. "Make a right there, on Pine Crest, and then follow it to Southwest Avenue. The prisoner stockade is at the rear of the hospital buildings, surrounded by barbed wire fencing. I'll call the Captain in charge to expect you in less than five."

When Franz and the others were later shown to what would be their "home" for the next sixteen months, he was pleasantly surprised at the simplistic, yet comfortably modernistic style of the accommodations. *These Americans certainly know how to take care of their "guests",* he thought, eyeing the newly built stockade with its five rows each of ten long, rectangular, brick barracks and squat wooden buildings. *This is so much better than the tents in Texas.*

Prodding them with their rifles, Lieutenant Quisling and Sergeant Cooper, who were to help guard the stockade, ushered the prisoners through the gates and indicated the buildings were mess halls, administration and supply huts, and PW camp commissaries. At the end, behind the fifth row was a small, squat brick chapel, with a short white, wooden spire topped by a silver-painted cross. Beside it was another small, long building that Cooper said was supposed to be a hospital for the prisoners.

"But it won't be used. If you get sick, there is a separate area set aside in a main building," he said, pointing to the back of a two-story brick structure. "You'll be well treated, just like our own patients..." he snorted. "Similar facilities, but separate. Just like the Conventions stipulate."

"And the doctors who will treat us?" a prisoner asked. From the accent, Franz surmised he was from Austria.

"Yours, of course," Quisling scoffed "Our guys are too busy helping our own wounded. There are not enough of us to go around to take care of them, let alone any of you. Which is why you all are here."

Assigned to Barracks 3, almost in the middle of the complex, Franz was not disappointed that the officer who had sat with him on the lorry was not going to be a bunkmate. Instead, all the twenty or so higher-ranking German soldiers in their contingent were to be housed in Barracks 1 and 2. The enlisted men, like Franz, were no longer going to be allowed to mingle with their superior officers. He was equally elated, however, that Staff Sergeant Otto Kempf was also considered an officer – *Probably more by rank, even if he was just an Oberfeldwebel, than by demeanor*, he surmised – and was assigned to live in Barracks 1. When the officers gathered their gear and were marched away, Franz hoped he would no longer have to deal with the slovenly rude medic.

SEVEN

Suzanne's best friend throughout her childhood and now on into adulthood was Peggy Holmes, a second generation Irish lass whose parents had immigrated to America from Blarney in the early 1920s during the last of the great potato famines.

An accomplished blacksmith, Peggy's father instantly found work in the Phoenixville Iron Works, pounding and shaping custom wrought-iron fences, gates, and doors that were incorporated into the luxurious homes newly being built all across the prosperous, burgeoning country.

When the Depression hit six years later, Shanney Holmes was laid off. But, undaunted and familiar with deprivation, he soon joined the Work Projects program sponsored by the U.S. government and helped to build railroads and subways.

When the war broke out, he was rehired by PIW and assigned to making weaponry and firearms of all shapes and sizes that were "sold" to England during the Lend Lease program and, later, when the United States finally entered the war in 1941, used by

American forces first in the European and then the Pacific theaters of operation.

Peggy was, as Suzanne also was of hers, inordinately proud of her father although she often called him, "a common laborer". Suzanne railed at this whenever Peggy said it, chiding her friend unmercifully until Peggy admitted that her father was not a laborer at all, "per se", but, in fact, a fine "artiste". Yet, with his gruff and almost crude mannerisms and faint Irish brogue, Shanney was less of a creative artist and more of a shanty Irishman – as his name implied – who angrily pounded his way through life upon the anvil of life's lost hopes and dreams. What he really wanted, despite their small, cramped, humble row home on Washington Street, was for Peggy, his only child, to be a "real proper young lady".

Shanney doted on his daughter and, in turn, grew to love, in his own way, Suzanne as his second child. He called the inordinately close friends his "twins". When the two of them huddled together in front of the Holmes' small wrought-iron fireplace grate – crafted, of course, by Shanney – on any given cold, wintery evening, he made it a point to sit with them for a while, regaling them both with his corny, trite Pat and Mike jokes and long, shaggy-dog stories of "the old sod".

While Peggy was duly embarrassed, Suzanne, in her own way, was beguiled. Mister Holmes had the same quirky sense of humor as her own father. Only more so. Shanney was more open, often boisterous, and very gregarious while Abram was quiet, wry, and reserved. Yet, both fiercely loving their daughters, they were very much alike. Suzanne often lamented to herself that it was a shame that she and Peggy were not members of the same church – she being a staunch Lutheran and her friend a strict Roman Catholic. Her father, she knew, would have loved to have Shanney as his friend.

But while Peggy was her best ever and dearest friend, Suzanne's mother was uneasy.

"I don't understand why you have to be caught up in the lives of that...that...rift-raft," Katerina Kessler often chided her daughter. "They are common...well, potato farming...*Irishmen*!"

"He's an accomplished blacksmith, Momma! Not a potato farmer," Suzanne once tried to protest, "And Peggy is my...*friend!*"

"Never you mind," Katerina stated, slamming the door on any further discussion or argument. "You know how I feel about you fraternizing with her...after school. Especially, with her father around! While you're at school, though...That...you know, is...well...different."

Suzanne didn't know and couldn't tell the difference. *A friend is a friend, regardless of age, religion, and/or ethical background*, she thought to herself. *I'll figure out a way.* She refrained from reminding her mother of their Germanic roots in a country with which their now *adoptive* country was at war.

Despite her mother's disapproval, Suzanne would often sneak out of the house in the early evenings, feigning trips to the library two blocks down across Main Street from their large three-story Victorian colonial. Instead of heading east, Peggy would walk in the opposite direction to Peggy's small house on Washington. She even lied about her after high school activities when Peggy and she would walk the long way home across Gay Street and wander through Morris Cemetery on Nutt Road across from the new pharmacy. Shuffling their way through the dusty autumn leaves, they made up stories about the names and dates engraved on the older gravestones. *He fought in the Revolutionary War and died at Valley Forge. This one was a soldier in the Civil War. She died of both love and cholera in 1918. Her husband was a great statesman. That one must have been a duke!*

Peggy was, for Suzanne, a creative inspiration and a loyal compatriot. Neither one was willing to give up their close camaraderie for anything. Not even Suzanne's mother...even if Katrina Kessler was hard-pressed to refrain from suggesting it.

That evening after dinner, having heard her father's rendition of the stirring war adventures of Sergeant John Voight and his descriptive, often humorous story of the arrival of the prisoners of war at the hospital that snowy morning – he had introduced himself as the "engineer who kept the six tall furnace towers straight" – Suzanne excused herself from the nightly family ritual of gathering around the large Philco radio in the second floor sitting room to listen to one of President Roosevelt's Fireside Chats and, bundled up with an extra sweater and scarf under her plaid woolen coat against the bitter cold and icy snow, silently slipped out of the house, turned left, and made her way in the dark toward Washington Street.

She just had to tell her best friend of all time about her newly discovered love whom she had just met that very morning. Sergeant Johnny...John Voight. The handsome ball turret gunner hero extraordinaire, who had, she finally and reluctantly admitted to herself, quickly captured her heart.

"He said that?" Peggy exuded, sitting cross-legged on her yellow and baby blue chenille bedspread. She was tall and prone to stockiness, with the typical Gallic brownish-red hair and profusion of tan freckles across her nose. Although born in the small bedroom of the apartment where her parents first lived after arriving in America and raised in Phoenixville, she spoke with her father's thick brogue. "He actually called you 'Susie'!?! Hadn't he the nerve!?!" she exclaimed, slightly trilling the "r" and lilting the end of her sentences.

"Yeah, but, strangely enough, I didn't mind...Despite his small, no...litheness. He is quite handsome and has this way...this manner...this sense of humor about him...Droll, like my father's. I kind of liked...like it. Being teased and all.

"That's not a'tall like you, Suzanne. Boy, are you smitten or what?!"

Suzanne blushed at her friend's comments. "Nyah...no way! Ya think?" she asked, despite knowing that what Peggy said was the truth.

At eighteen, she had no real experience with men nor any real idea of what "falling in love" was to feel like. She had on occasion casually dated a few boys in high school, but that's what they were. Boys. Not mature, grown men like John Voight who was six years her senior and a wounded veteran of war.

"'Course I do. Why else would you brave this snowstorm to tell me about him? When a simple phone call would have sufficed?" Peggy turned and looked out her bedroom window. Large snowflakes were falling in think clumps, splattered by the wind against the glass, piling up on the sill and occluding the top panes.

"It's really coming down. Hard and fast. Kinda like you've fallen for..."

"Don't even say it!" Suzanne interrupted her

friend. She grabbed her coat, sweaters, and scarves. "I don't want to hear it! Besides, I should head back before it...the weather gets any worse and my parents..."

"You can't go out in that!" Peggy exclaimed.

"What? The storm? Or my coat?" she asked, wrapping the beaver collar tightly around her neck.

"Despite its thickness...it's still not enough. You'd be buried beneath a drift or worse...frozen to death for sure...even before you've a chance to cross Gay Street! You just have to stay here. At least until the storm clears..."

"I can't...my mother..."

"When is she ever going to accept...finally acknowledge that we are best, inseparable friends? Forever. Just like she once was with my mother..."

"What?" Suzanne asked in disbelief.

"What? You don't know? She didn't tell you?" Peggy smirked. "It was, probably still would have been the friendship of a lifetime. Had not I..." She stopped. Despite being the cause of her mother's death, it wasn't her place, or her secret to tell.

Suzanne glared at her friend, puzzled. She tried to shake off the sad feeling that Peggy did not have the benefit of growing up with both parents. She and her father, however, had made more than just the best of it.

"Make do with what you have," Shanney kept on saying, providing adequately for his only child. Both he and Peggy, it seemed to Suzanne, were quite content and happy, despite the lack of a wife and mother. Yet, she couldn't help the occasional twinges of pity. At least she had her own mother, however strict, harsh, and formidable she might be at times.

She looked away from Peggy and stared out the window, watching the white flakes grow larger and larger as they densely fell, completely obliterating the small lawn in front of the Holmes' row house and the street beyond. She knew it would be impossible to walk back up Washington, across Gay, and down Second Avenue to her own home that evening. Peggy was right. She'd be smothered and frozen inside of five minutes. Instead, she acquiesced and asked to use the phone.

"Momma?" she pleaded into the cordite mouthpiece. 'I, um... I am..."

"Where are you?" Katrina Kessler asked, gripping the receiver tightly against her ear. She had just now gone up to Suzanne's second floor bedroom to wish her a "good night" and, realizing her daughter was not in bed and nowhere else in the house, had begun to panic. "I am so worried."

"Don't do that, Momma," Suzanne whispered. "I am at...Well, I am at Peggy's. Safe and sound. And warm. I snuck out to visit her after dinner...and with this storm...I need to stay here. At least until the morning"

"What?! But..."

"I know, Momma...but she *is* my best friend." Suzanne paused. "Just like you and Mrs. Holmes were. Why didn't you tell me? Instead of chastising me all the time?"

Her mother fell silent on the other end of the line. All Suzanne could hear were the slight, panting exhalations of her mother's sighs.

"Momma? Are you there? Are you alright?"

"It's a long story. About Peggy's mother. I...can't talk about it." Even after all these years since her untimely death, she still couldn't bring herself to utter the name of her closest friend. She cleared her throat with a soft guttural sound, trying to hide the catch in her voice. "You missed a second helping of dessert after Roosevelt's chat…"

"We're okay. Mr. Holmes brought us tea and homemade lemon scones with boysenberry jam, my favorite…Who knew Mr. Holmes was such a good baker!?"

"Don't talk to me of Shanney Holmes!" her mother growled into the phone. "That Irish scallywag!" She smothered the phone between her small breasts to collect and calm her thoughts.

"Mother?" The silence on the other end was deafening.

"Fine," Katerina said finally. "With the snow piling up, there is no way you can make it home safely. But you shouldn't have snuck out in the first place…Against my wishes…"

"I know, Momma. I am sorry…but…"

"Fine. It's done. No need to explain any further…"

"Then can I stay?"

"Of course. Of course, you may stay. With this weather, you'll have to. You are an adult now. You make your own decisions. If that is what you…you want…you need to do."

"No, Momma…It is what it is…What it must be."

"Goodnight, Suzanne," her mother said. Then, quietly, she whispered "I...um, I love you."

"Me, too, Momma. Good night."

Early the next morning, Suzanne braved the cold and the last vestiges of the snowstorm and walked the three-quarters of a mile back to her home. She quickly changed into suitable clothes for work and donned her woolen plaid beaver fur collared long coat. She was about to leave when her father called from the kitchen.

"No use, Suzanne! Just heard on the radio that the streets are clogged with snow and jammed with stranded cars. Buses are delayed, if they're running at all. Hell of a storm. Best you stay home today..."

In a way, Suzanne was relieved. She and Peggy had stayed up most of the night talking about John and the newly arrived prisoners of war at the army hospital. She was tired and could use a day of rest. Yet, she was also eager to get back to work. To once again be with the new, charming shipping clerk.

But that, she sighed, *would have to wait until tomorrow.*

EIGHT

While reasonably well-fed at the behest of the United States government during his last two years held captive in Camp Mexia in Texas, Franz had still lost a bit of weight. He attributed his loss of appetite to being homesick for Eisenach and worrying about his mother and, of course, Greta.

In the beginning of his stay, he wrote the allotted two weekly letters home, enclosing his missives to Greta in the envelopes addressed to his mother. And while they had at first faithfully replied with short, cryptic sentences relating the many hardships under the Third Reich – a dire shortage of food and the commandeering of most of their farm animals for the war effort – he hadn't heard from them in over a year. Franz, now nearly frantic with concern, still continued to write his long weekly letters, not knowing if they even did reach his mother or whether she was still living on the farm.

There was also no word from Greta. He prayed nightly that she was still safe in his mother's care and had not yet been found.

Now a bit frailer and thinner than when he first arrived in the United States, Franz had caught a bad cold. *Probably,* he thought, *from riding in the open lorry in the middle of the snowstorm.* A few days after arriving at camp and settling into Barracks 3, he started sneezing. When a racking cough developed, he was ordered to the prisoner's hospital ward where, wrapped in scratchy U.S. Army blankets, he huddled in a bed next to a large steam radiator.

It was two weeks before he was well enough to take up his tasks working on the hospital wards. He spent his days studying a battered, dog-eared German-to-English dictionary one of the kindly guards at Camp Texia had given him, sipping strong coffee and noshing on buttered mashed potatoes riddled with chunks of bratwurst.

While Franz was in the hospital, the rest of the German prisoners busied themselves with organizing the social and political structure in the stockade; as was the custom under the Geneva Conventions for most of the other PW camps across the country. They had been given almost free rein by Captain Charles Templeton, the prison Camp Commander, for their own governance. More than half of the prisoners, mostly officers, including the zealot Otto Kempf, were pro-Nazi. They used their "superior" influence to emulate and recreate an atmosphere and culture in all of the barracks that paralleled the Nazi regime, enforcing National Socialistic ideology and demanding strict adherence to Hitler's dreams, wishes, and tenets. Anyone who defied the "status quo" by talking about democracy, reading American newspapers, or listening to the radio was considered a United States sympathizer – a traitor, secretly and summarily court-martialed at night, severely punished, and, though rarely, executed.

The 1929 Geneva Conventions allowed for the prisoners to elect a liaison – an *Unteroffizier* – between the prisoners and their American captors. Otto, much to Franz's dismay when he learned about it later, bullied his way into being elected to the position. In his new position, the Staff Sergeant was tasked with bringing grievances and "unfair" treatment that the prisoners thought violated the Conventions to the attention of Captain Templeton. If he was not satisfied with the result, Kempf had the right, on behalf of the prisoners – as well as the authority – to contact the International Red Cross who, in turn, notified the Swiss Legation, the neutral agency that acted as the conduit of information from the United States to Germany. It was only a matter of time before Herr Sergeant *Unteroffizier* Kempf began to abuse his new-found power, taking total control of how he thought the prisoners should think, feel, and act.

All of this, Franz knew, would profoundly affect him and, in time, a few others. Had he been at the meeting when Otto was chosen, he would have adamantly voiced his objections. *He's a poor example of what a true German is,* Franz said almost out loud to himself. *Besides being crude, rude, and mean-spirited, he doesn't even speak English. And the Commander does not speak a word of German. How could they communicate without a translator? Perhaps, when I am better, I could do that...*

But, for now, except for the news of the election of the liaison, he decided to keep out of Otto's way lest he discover Franz's growing fondness for all things American. It was best for now to remain vaguely unaware and unconcerned about what was happening outside his hospital room and concentrate on getting well. Franz was anxious to begin his duties nursing wounded American soldiers in the ophthalmology ward.

During Franz's confinement, the doctor who had tried to befriend him during their cold ride through Phoenixville visited a few times.

"I'm on duty in orthopedics," he explained the first time. "Herr Doctor Kraus said you had a bad cold, so I brought you some home-made chicken soup." He smiled and put a large ceramic mug alongside the old German-to-English dictionary splayed open on the small table next to Franz's bed. "I made it last night in the camp kitchen. My mother's own age-old home recipe is much more effective than today's modern medicine."

Franz wanly smiled his thanks, curious as to why the officer was being so friendly toward him.

"How are you feeling?" he asked, pulling up an old, white-painted wooden office chair next to Franz's bed.

"Better," Franz said cryptically. He still wasn't sure whether the sub-lieutenant could be trusted. Even if he was a doctor. Even physicians can be duplicitous.

"Well, you've heard about Otto?"

"Yes...but I, er," Franz wanted to vent his pent-up frustrations and objections, but until he knew the doctor could be relied upon to keep his confidences, he would keep his own feelings to himself.

"It is a shame. A man like that. Despite him being an officer and a medic. We should have someone more...professional to represent us," the doctor said. "I would have offered, but my long shifts helping the other surgeons on the ward. Well, I would not have had the time."

"Do you speak English? We need someone who could speak fluent English. At least be able to translate."

"Ah, *ja*. But I do..." The doctor smiled again, nodding at the splayed dictionary. "And I see that you do, too..."

"A bit. I am...learning." Franz paused, and then said tentatively, "You won't tell...Otto on me, would you?"

"*Oh, Mein Freund yonng. Nein, nein*...No, my young friend. I will not tell. What Otto doesn't hear about or know is best for him. And for us. Eh, Franz Weberhardt?"

"*Danke.*"

"Oh, I almost forgot," the doctor said, taking a small sketch pad, two lead pencils, and a brown rubber eraser out of his white coat pocket and putting them on the blanket. "I know you like to draw...that you are somewhat of an artist. So I brought you something to draw with."

Franz scooted up in bed, half sitting, half reclining against the pillow and picked up the pad.

"*Danke, Herr Doktor.* Er, Sir. Very thoughtful. I will put them to good use. But..." Franz stumbled over his words during a racking bout of coughing and sneezing. "I feel uncomfortable calling you '*Herr Doktor*', even though you are one. But, excuse me, but...might I know your name, since you already know mine?"

"Ah...Yes. That is most fair. No, I guess I didn't tell you, did I? Sorry...It's...Well..." he hedged, smoothing a non-existent wrinkle on a starched sleeve of his smock. Despite his duties as the assistant to one of the American orthopedic surgeons, large blue PW letters were stitched on its back and both arms. "Do you want both of them?"

"You have two names?"

"Well…yes. My real one and the one I adopted before the Nazis found me out." He paused. "The one I gave them when I was forced into the medical corps."

"The one you…adopted?" Franz was intrigued. Perhaps there was more to this sub-lieutenant who persisted in wanting to be his friend. And who seemed to want to share a secret. Perhaps he could be trusted after all. "Both please. If you don't mine. Sir."

"Well, I am known as *Zweiter Leutnant Zur See…Herr Doktor* Zoloff. But in my former life, my real name…was…" he paused, intently staring at Franz, "…Samuel Goldberg."

"What?" Franz sat up straighter and began coughing again. He couldn't quite phantom what the doctor was telling him. "You. Are. Jewish?!" he exclaimed. *Like Greta,* he thought. *Hence, the homemade chicken soup.*

"Shush. Walls have ears. Like the Americans say. Loose lips sink ships," the doctor smiled. "No one but you here now knows that. No one must know. Please don't tell anyone," he pleaded. "If the other prisoners knew…and Otto found out…"

"They would kill you," Franz spat out. "Don't worry. You can trust me. But...how?" Franz sputtered as he coughed. "How? I thought you were a...a Lutheran!"

""Easy, now, my son," Goldberg, alias Zoloff chortled, patting Franz's blanket. "Yes, in a sense I am...But that was...is only a ruse. There, now. Don't talk." He handed Franz the mug of soup. "Here, have some of this. It will help the phlegm work its way out."

"How did a...*Jüdischen*...a Jew get into the German army?"

"It's a long story...but these unbelievable things do happen," he laughed again. "Even in Nazi Germany."

"I was born and raised as Samuel Goldberg on the outskirts of Wien – the Americans know it better as Vienna – in a small hamlet called Wolstenholtz. My father, as his father before him, was a prosperous merchant. For many, many centuries, even through the last...the Great War...it was a quiet, peaceful town. Pastoral. Untouched by anything, not even by the outside world except the occasional storm...the forces of nature.

"Very much like your own home…Eisenach. Wolstenholtz was quite like that. We kept our own old ways, following our own traditions. Even had our own set of laws – *ein Code of Ethics*, as it were. Anyway…Nothing disturbed us until March of 1938 when Hitler and his armies invaded and took over our country. The Anschluss. I had already graduated from the medical school at Berlin University and was about to join a private practice in Vienna…when we were almost, literary, wiped out.

"The rest…We were forced to flee our homes. Hours, sometimes minutes before the soldiers marched into them, taking, destroying, and ruining everything in sight. Because, you see, they were looking for Jews and someone had…What is the American equivalent for *Ratted uns aus*…Squealed? Look it up in your dictionary."

"Ratted you out?" Franz stated after a moment of thumbing through the battered, green cloth-bound book.

"Yes. That is right. As for me, my family, you might ask…My parents and I, my younger sister, Helga, and our family dog – a lumbering Doberman

Pincher we named Pirat – were lucky to escape to the countryside. But it was as if the Nazis already knew who of us in the village were Jewish and were to be rounded up and killed first before...the rest. We were the lucky ones."

This is Verboten, Franz thought, for *this man – Manheim/Samuel – to be telling me his life's story.* According to the Hitler Youth Movement dogma he had been forced to learn, it was forbidden in the *Wehrmacht Medical Korps* to discuss anything personal between themselves other than the care of their wounded.

But they were now here, in America, where freedom of speech was a commonplace guarantee and not a punishable crime, despite the pro-Nazi culture that was preserved and now persisted throughout the prison barracks.

"Afraid for our safely, my father valiantly coaxed us all further into the woods away from the sound of the guns and tanks rumbling through the streets of our village, destroying everything in their way."

"But I thought...the Anschluss was peaceful," Franz protested. 'The newspapers said...'

"Pure propaganda. A number of Austrian towns

and villages were destroyed before the others capitulated. Vienna, however it is true, was, of course, spared. Most of it, anyway. It was to be a prized jewel in Hitler's crown. A symbol of his Aryan culture. But the Jews living there...we...they were captured in droves.

"After three days of sleeping on pine needles and only eating what we could forage, we stumbled upon a large farmhouse nestled deep in the woods, near the foothills of the Alps. In desperation, cold and hungry, we knocked on the door hoping those inside were not Nazi sympathizers."

"And...Where they?"

"To our delight and surprise," *Herr Doktor* smiled at the memories. "The Zoloff's were a kind and generous Lutheran family who took us in, hid us in their barn for a few days, and then 'adopted' us as their own. They did not care if we were Jewish. They only cared for our – and their – safety. They simply asked that we not mention nor practice our religion or discuss our different cultural mores ever again. At least while we were in their home. My father, of course, was livid and very nearly refused. But knowing we wouldn't be safe if we did continue to openly live our faith, he acquiesced. We changed our name to theirs, pretended to adopt their religion, and worked alongside them on the farm.

"I assisted with the animals, applying my medical knowledge to their needs. My mother and sister took to cooking, baking, churning butter, and to sewing. And Pirat delighted in cavorting with the Zoloff's own dogs. All was peaceful...almost like Wolstenholtz was before the, um, invasion. But the threat of being discovered always loomed like a dark shadow over our shoulders.

"Finally, late one afternoon as we were just about to eat an early supper, there was a loud knock on the door. Herr Zoloff was reluctant to answer it, but my father, while hoping against hope, was resigned to his and his family's eventual fate.

"'Let them in,' he said. 'We've been here two years already...Borrowed time. There is no place else to go and it would be suspicious if no one answered.'

"But, you see, it wasn't the *Geheime Staatspolizei* – the Gestapo – nor the *Spionagedienst* – the Secret Service – but two regular army officers who had come to claim the Zoloff's son for the *Wehrmacht*.

"Erik, the oldest, for whatever reasons had been

able to avoid joining the Hitler Youth Movement. But now, he was instantly conscripted.

"They also asked about one 'Manheim Zoloff' – that was, is me. When I told them I was actually a doctor, they asked to see my credentials. But, you see, they – hidden under the floorboards in my room – had my former Jewish name on them. I was forced to lie. I told them they were lost in a fire, hoping they would believe me and not ask any further questions.

"Both Erik and I were hauled off that night...allowed only the briefest of good-byes...and driven to the nearest army camp. Erik was instantly given a uniform and a rifle and shipped to the Russian front. I was taken to Berlin where I was forced to again take the two-day exams to prove I was, indeed, a *doktor*. I, of course, passed, was given a certificate with my right...'correct' name on it...inducted into the *Medizinkorps*, and, well, as you can see. Here I am."

Franz had quietly sat wide-eyed during Manheim's recitation. He was amazed that a farming family in the countryside had so willingly taken the Goldbergs in. Imagine! The near stupidity of the

German officers who believed – without asking how, when, or where – Zoloff's ruse about loosing his papers in a fire made him chuckle. But more ironic was that a Jewish countryman was serving as a high-ranking officer – a doctor! – in the German army!

Well, as he had said, "These unbelievable things do happen...even in Nazi Germany."

"So, um," Franz asked quietly. "What do I call you? Samuel or Manheim?"

"Manheim for now, please. But once, hopefully, we...Hitler looses this inane war and we are repatriated, you must call me Samuel. Just remember, it's my...now our little secret."

Franz nodded. After hearing *Herr Doktor* Goldberg/Zoloff's story, he wanted to share his tale...of Greta. *Mother had been hiding her for months before I left,* he thought. *I hope that she would still be safely living there when I return.* But he refrained from saying anything. It was not the right time to share his own troubled memories.

"Yes...Manheim," he promised. "I will not tell anyone. You can trust me."

"Yes, Franz. I do. With my life."

NINE

During the two weeks it took for his cold to slowly dissipate, Franz had substantially added new English words, terms, and phrases to his repertoire. Not quite fluent, he able to more effectively communicate with the guards and, when he was finally well enough to work a full eight hour daily shift as a nurse in the hospital, he could somewhat effectively communicate with the patients. The more he talked with the Americans, the more proficient he became. By the end of March, he was proficient enough to be a translator for the other prisoners; a service well received by their guards who were frustrated at not being able to understand and be understood by their charges. He was even able, on the rare occasion, to assist Otto, the camp *Unteroffizier,* when he was required to talk with Captain Templeton.

To his delight, Franz was assigned to one of the ophthalmology wards. During his first and, so far, only year of medicine at Efburt University, he had been fascinated by the construction and workings of the eye, although his studies had been cut short by conscription into Hitler's war. Now, in America, he had a second chance.

Among his various duties he readily and eagerly changed head and eye bandages, carefully inserted and maintained IVs, bathed patients, and, under the supervision of U.S. Army doctors and nurses, administered the intricate doses of the various prescribed medicines. He was thrilled that he could utilize the skills he had learned during his year of medical school as well as those learned as a medic in the field of battle.

He closely watched the American doctors and surgeons, avid to absorb as much as he could to advance his own knowledge. He knew he had a lot to learn, but by astutely studying American techniques now, he had hopes that he would be fully prepared, should he later have the opportunity to return home and continue studying medicine at the university.

As the weeks passed, Franz learned the names and histories of many of the patients. They came to know and trust the young, eager German, a prisoner turned nurse who spoke nearly fluent English. They were open and honest about discussing their thoughts and fears for the future with him and amongst themselves.

However pleased he was working with the patients, Franz was more than dismayed at the extent of the injuries suffered during battle by the men he no longer considered "the enemy". Many, if not all of the patients had been partially or fully blinded during battle, losing their sight and often their hearing to concussive head trauma from the loud, exploding cannons; gunshot wounds to the head; and retinal nerve damage from other serious cranial wounds. Franz was devastated by the extent of their injuries; the length of the proscribed recovery time; the dim view of most of the blind men who were doubtful they would ever be able to continue living a full life.

What appalled him the most, however, were the effects of exposure to the residual chemicals released when bombs from both sides exploded. He had been told through the *Wehrmacht* propaganda machine that filtered news down to his unit in Italy that Germany had willingly complied with the Treaty of Versailles after World War I and agreed not to use chemical warfare of any kind. The American doctors and nurses concurred; it was true. In point of fact, Hitler had absolutely refused their use. But as he tended to the soldiers who had lost their sight because of the severe burns induced by fire contacting their skins, Franz realized that the injuries were just as bad. Franz had no words for his anger and disgust at the cruel, inhumanity of war and his fellow Germans. There was no way to express – in either German or his newly learned English – his utter disappointed in the shear cruelty and total lack of respect for other human beings on both sides, even if they were "the enemy".

He prayed silently, as he tried to tenderly care for those in his charge, that the Allies, even if they, too, were complacent in using needlessly dangerous weapons, would prevail and soon bring Hitler down, stopping his rampant rampaging rape of the world. He knew that his new friend, Manheim, working almost day and night in another ward to save the battered limbs of other American soldiers, felt the same way.

He was not so sure about the rest of the prisoners.

Franz was bemused one day to see Otto on what he came to call "his" ward scrubbing floors, cleaning toilets, and washing bedpans. Despite all his bravado demanding respect as Staff Sergeant Herr Kempf, "the medic" – even though he had been elected as the *Unteroffizier* – had been demoted, much to his chagrin, to what he considered the "lowly" status of orderly.

Such is the fate of a prisoner of war, Franz smiled to himself. *Serves him right.* But when, as if reading his thoughts, Otto caught his eye and gestured lewdly, Franz quickly turned his back and pretended he did not see. *No sense in getting involved with his kind,* he thought. *Best,* as he had a while ago promised himself, *to stay clear of the miscreant as best I can and leave him well enough alone. Even if I am asked to translate for him...*

Since the arrival of the prisoners and the election of the *Unteroffizier* the American guards did not interfere with what went on in the German living quarters. Otto and other more outspoken prisoners continued to insist that strict adherence be kept to the tenets of Hitler's regime. As a result, all of the barracks in the stockade, including Barracks 3, were totally immersed in Nazi culture.

Despite the offering of American newspapers and books, the pro-Nazi prisoners refused the "falsified democracy propaganda" and frowned upon others who were eager to learn more about the culture of their captors. Unlike Franz and, he suspected, a number of others, many still believed – despite the massive European invasion of American troops on June 6, 1944 – that Germany would decisively win the war and occupy the United States. These prisoners jeered and taunted their captors, sneering that while they were prisoners now, the tables will soon be turned and the guards would be the ones behind barbed wire. Anyone who dared to defy the pro-Nazis were summarily ignored and, as the days and weeks wore on, secretly and severely punished.

Ten

The first Saturday morning when the Reverend Fromüeller arrived on the VFGH complex and was introduced to the prisoners by Captain Templeton as their chaplain, he was rebuffed.

"I doubt very much anyone here would go for that," the *Unteroffizier* sneered, surprised that the large, burly man who claimed to be a minister spoke fluent German. "Especially us officers."

"How about we ask them? And the enlisted men, as well..."

"I am the person who makes the decisions around here. "

"But..."

"We all believe in Nazism," Otto continued in German, refusing to allow the minister to say anything further. "It is our one, true ideology and the only theology we need. So, I suggest you pack up your little liturgical bag and go home."

But the Lutheran minister was adamant.

"The German prisoners have the right to decide for themselves, even if you are...What's your name?"

"Otto Kempf," he mockingly spat out.

"That may be all very well, Otto. Even if you are their representative. But I have a letter authorizing me…"

"I don't care. There will be no church worship services here."

The reverend squared back his massive, bear-like shoulders.

"I will be in the chapel every Saturday morning at ten, Otto. You do realize you have an obligation…No, a responsibility as their, um, leader, under the auspices of the International Red Cross, to tell the prisoners this.

"You need not come yourself," Pastor Freddy stated emphatically. "But I will gladly welcome anybody else who so freely wishes to come worship with me."

Otto Kempf resented being told of his duties as the camp liaison, but he did not want to be accused of not following the IRC guidelines. Hitler, he knew, had been quite adamant about following most of them, as well as those of the Geneva Conventions, to the letter.

"Suit yourself," the *Unteroffizier* smirked again.

That evening during the prisoners' mess, Otto did reluctantly tell the other captives about the Lutheran services that would start next Saturday in the small chapel. But, expressing his disapproval and reminding them of their pro-Nazi tenets and where their true loyalties must lie, he strongly cautioned everybody not to attend.

The next week, the Reverend Fromüeller stood in front of the altar draped in a long, white embroidered cloth and looked out onto his new second congregation. Only one of the prisoners had come.

Franz Weberhardt sat, hymnal in hand, expectantly, eagerly awaiting the service to start.

When the tall, hefty pastor kindly smiled at him, he smiled back.

Eleven

When word spread throughout the camp that President Franklin Delano Roosevelt had succumbed to a cerebral hemorrhage on April 12, 1945 many of the pro-Nazis cheered. They knew that FDR was the primary force behind the American troops that invaded German strongholds in Europe, almost now certain to destroy Hitler and his Third Reich. With Roosevelt dead and Harry S. Truman, whom they thought would be his weak successor, as president, the prisoners, especially the officers – as well as Otto – were convinced that the tides would turn back to Germany's favor.

Franz was convinced otherwise. While working on the wards, he listened to the American broadcasts the patients had tuned to on their radios, hearing more and more of the many Allied successes in battle. How the U.S. Army was marching closer and closer to Berlin; how the German *Wehrmacht* was sulking farther and farther from the front; how Paris was finally loosening the bonds of invasion and occupation.

"Won't be long, now," one patient smiled. "Hitler's bound to crack...And our boys can finally come home. Whoops, sorry, Franz. I almost didn't, um, see you there. No offense..."

"None taken. Just because I am a German doesn't mean I believe in...all that Nazi nonsense," Franz stated in perfect English. Then, instantly realizing his mistake in speaking out: "I am sorry. I shouldn't have said that."

"No, it's okay. Quite refreshing, actually. To hear one of whom we think is the enemy...not believe in...how do you say it in German? The cause?"

"*Der Sache...der Nazis...*"

"Yeah, that. And you don't believe...?"

"*Nein*. Never have." He paused. "And never will."

"Well, that's good to hear! Ain't it, guys?"

Franz was taken aback with the ensuing round of applause.

Tonight, he thought, *I will sketch for them a portrait of their deceased president...to say...Danke schön!*

The next morning, the charcoal sketch of FDR was proudly taped up onto the wall next to the bed of a young Merchant Marine's who had lost an eye and was partially blind in the other. When another patient described the sketch and the fine details in it to him, Tom complimented Franz.

"It's really good, my young friend. Really good. You certainly do have talent. I used to draw a lot," he said as he fumbled for the leather case stowed in the small, white metal cabinet next to his bed. "Here. You might as well have these." He gingerly touched the gauze bandage thickly wrapped around his head and over his eyes. "I have no more use for them, now. Especially since I completely lost my left one...And it looks as if you will put them to much better use."

The satchel was filled with colored drawing pencils, charcoal sticks, erasers, a tin of oil paints and brushes, and a large sketch pad. On its first few pages were finely etched, detailed renditions of ships sinking at sea, smoke billowing from bombed smoke stacks; men in fraying life-jackets clinging to splintered keels of lifeboats in the midst of burning oil slicking around them; buildings in ruins; soldiers scrambling over hillsides and into forests under dark plumes of gun smoke and shell fire; army tents strewn across a meadow behind the front lines;

tanks barreling through marshes and muddy creeks strewn with the wounded and the dead – German, Italian, American soldiers alike.

"These are very good, Tom," Franz said. "I draw...but not this well."

"I tried to capture the brutal essence of the war, hoping to capture what I..." there was a slight catch in his voice, "...what I saw. On sea and, later, on land...I thought that one, maybe one day, I'd do a whole book...of my war memories so that people will remember..."

"You should keep them. Perhaps, someday, you will see again with the one eye and be able to..."

"No! The doctors say my nerves are damaged beyond repair. I can only see some light and faint shadows. And my confidence, walking around with an ugly empty socket, is totally gone. I know with the scarred and sunken eyelid, I look hideous. But, you seem sensitive enough to understand. Do me a favor. You take the paper and pencils and charcoal. Use them well. Now that I can't."

Tom reached up and groped until he could place his hand on Franz's shoulder. "Draw what you see here. What you remember back home. Then you can show, er, describe to me what you've done…your pictures. Okay?"

"Sure," Franz smiled. "This gift to me is the greatest of honors." He hoped his words conveyed the deep, grateful emotion that swelled in his heart.

"Now…do a portrait of one of your own German heroes."

"I don't have any German heroes…None from the war, anyway."

"Then do one of someone you truly admire. I am sure there is such a person…"

"*Ja*, Oh, yes. There certainly is," Franz said, thinking of the young man sequestered in the castle fortress nearly four centuries ago.

"But I did not known him…Personally, that is. Just the stories of him. He lived in our small German town…Many, many years ago. And there are legends."

"That doesn't matter," Tommy said. "You admire him just the same?"

"Oh, yes," Franz grinned. "Very much."

"Then he is the subject of your next painting."

Ever since that afternoon, Franz toted Tom's leather case with him everywhere. When and where he could, he sketched, capturing his own thoughts and memories into pictures; pouring his thoughts and feelings into his visual depictions.

But now that he had the supplies he needed, and Tommy's urging, the project the young German prisoner really wanted to tackle was an oil painting of Martin Luther sitting in the courtyard of the Wartburg castle fortress.

TWELVE

Despite keeping the strict pro-Nazi regimen, many of the prisoners indulged themselves in hobbies and sports, quickly forming soccer teams and playing Saturday morning matches on the makeshift field in back of the barracks. Some of the prisoners were accomplished musicians and had been members of orchestras at other prisoner of war camps. They formed a small dance band and practiced in the arts and crafts building, hoping to play a concert or two for an audience of both the PWs and the hospital patients. On any given Saturday or Sunday afternoon, strains of "Lily Marlene" could be heard wafting over the PW camp and through the open windows of the hospital, delighting not only the displaced Germans, but the patients, as well.

Even gruff Otto enjoyed the music, although he did not admit it to anyone else but himself. The German ballad was his favorite song from home. Much to the annoyance of his bunkmates, he often loudly whistled it in the evenings, slightly out of tune, over and over and over again.

Franz knew enough to keep his anti-Nazi, pro-democratic, and, now, religious thoughts to himself, spending as much of his free time as he could away from his pro-Nazi bunkmates. In the evening, after a light supper, he read books borrowed from the small library set up in one corner of the camp canteen by representatives of the International Red Cross. On Saturday mornings he faithfully joined Reverend Fromüeller in worship and on Sunday afternoons he did his laundry.

Each early evening, weather permitting, he strolled around the inner perimeter of the stockade looking for a suitable spot to sit and sketch memories of the pre-war Wartburg countryside. He also began sketching a large, rough study of the portrait, trying to image what the finished painting would look like.

Yet, as much as he tried to remain aloof and apart from the pro-Nazi prisoners, Franz did have to share the same quarters with them at night. He could not help hearing about the "incidences" whispered between the beds as the men sought sleep.

Within the short two months since the prisoners had arrived at the Valley Forge General Hospital compound, there were various clandestine "trials" and subsequent punishments of anti-Nazi prisoners. Already, there had been two "suspicious" beatings of fellow prisoners who, like himself, had futilely tried to stay away from the Nazi tyrants.

Unteroffizier Herr Otto Kempf was the camp's most fanatic proponent of the pro-Nazi movement, inciting the now almost nightly uprisings and presiding over the secret "trials".

THIRTEEN

Later that month, Manheim, whom Franz rarely saw now that both of them were assigned to different wards, told him during a brief encounter while walking back from a rare afternoon shift together, that Otto was actually suspected of murdering – by brute force, no less, in the dead of the night – a much older anti-Nazi American sympathizer as he was making his way back from the latrines.

The victim had been a renowned specialist in dermatology back in Vienna before the war and had been teaching the American doctors a skin graft procedure he had effectively used in a German field hospital for burn victims. He was "accused" in abstentia during a secret trial held late one night in back of the stockade of being a loud, vocal adversary of the Nazi movement. His major crime was his often vocal decrying to the American doctors and guards of the current trend of pro-Hitler prisoners ruling the barracks with "a cruel German fist in a dirty iron glove".

"His body," Manheim whispered, "was found crumpled against a brick corner of the commissary. The right side of his head was bashed in." Apparently, the talented dermatologist had lost his way in the dark, became disoriented, and simply, without knowing it was there, walked straight into the wall. No one said anything different, but everyone Manheim had spoken to had the feeling he was murdered.

"Many of us in Barracks 1 heard the doctor get up in the middle of the night to use the latrine. A few minutes later, Kempf also got up and stormed out the door, cursing that he, too, '...badly had to go...' A half hour later, he came back alone. Our fellow *doktor* did not return..."

"Who found him?" Franz inquired. "The doctor...?"

"One of the guards. Lieutenant Quisling, I think, who stumbled upon him during an early morning camp patrol. Nothing else was further said. But with a head wound like that...just blindly walking into a wall...I don't know." He paused, frowned, and then, pulling Franz close, whispered, "I actually believe that Otto had also gotten up in the middle of the night with the sole purpose – as *Unteroffizier* – of killing the doctor."

"I thought we were sent the cream of the crop," Colonel Henry Beakers, who was serving, because of the shortage of Army personal stateside, in dual positions as the Post Commander and Chief Medical Officer, asked when Captain "Ernie" Templeton told him later that afternoon of the incident. "Deaths of those in captivity should be expected. But walking into a wall in the dark of night? Inexplicable. The camp grounds are well lighted, are they not?"

"Not enough, Sir. The camp, except for the sweeping spotlights, is mostly dark at night." Captain Templeton fidgeted as he stood at attention, realizing he had just inanely stated the obvious.

"You're the Camp Commander, for God's sake. You're supposed to be in charge of the prisoners! This should not have happened!" He slammed a fist down on the large mahogany desk, recently sanded and polished by one of the prisoners to a mirrored shine.

He glared at Captain Templeton, looking for answers.

"I suspect foul play. Those pro-Nazis I imagine. Weren't they weaned out during the culling to find German medical personnel to help us?"

"Yes, Sir. But more than a few got through. Those Germans are wily, Sir. Quite adept at convincingly lying through their teeth, especially when there's a chance of being moved to a smaller camp with better facilities and a higher standard of living..."

"Geezus!" Beakers swore under his breath. "As usual, incompetent interrogation. I was very adamant about not having any fanatical Nazi zealots here. What the hell happened?"

"As I said, Sir. Accomplished liars."

"Did you conduct an investigation?"

"Yes, Sir. But it revealed nothing. When I questioned them – using that young Weberhardt as the translator – none of the officers said anything more than they heard the doctor get up and leave Barracks 1, followed by Otto a few minutes later. And Sergeant Kempf was more taciturn than usual, claiming he had a touch of dysentery and it was just a coincidence that he got up at the same time as the older officer.

"'I saw nothing, did nothing...I quickly used the facilities and then returned to my bunk,'" he told me. At least that's what the translator said he said..."

"And no one saw Otto with the physician? A guard, perhaps? Another prisoner?"

"It was the dead of night, Sir...Nobody was around."

"Damn. Even if he did do it, we have no proof." Colonel Beakers dismissed Templeton with a wave of his darkly-tanned hand. "Well, there is nothing more we can do, is there? I guess we'll have to call this case closed. But, should anything further like this happen, Ernie ...You're outta here. Got that?"

"Yes, Sir!"

"And, by the way, try to get that trouble-making Sergeant Otto Kempf transferred!" the colonel yelled, once again slamming his fist on the desk.

"But he's their *Unteroffizier*...Our liaison..."

"I don't care who he is. I don't want him or any of his kind within fifteen miles of my patients!"

Captain Templeton snapped to attention

"Yes, Sir! I'll figure out a way! At once, Sir!"

He saluted smartly, and then turned on his heels and quickly walked out of the office.

FOURTEEN

While whispered rumors of murder circulated throughout the camp, they soon dissipated when the case of the "innocent but unfortunate" death was closed for lack of "sufficient" evidence to convict the *Unteroffizier.* Franz had later learned to his dismay, that no one, even any of the more "honorable officers" – not even Manheim – were brave enough, fearing retaliation from Otto and his fanatical group of pro-Nazis, to come forward and testify against him. No one had stepped up to vindicate the brutal, sad, and lonely death of their colleague, the older, much admired physician.

While he had, in fact, gotten away with it, Otto suspected that Captain Templeton, as well as the majority of his fellow prisoners, still suspected he was responsible for the death of the German *Herr Doktor.* The Camp Commander, he knew, was still looking for tangible proof besides mistrust and suspicion to have him transported to Fort Leavenworth, where both convicted Americans and prisoners of war were sent.

Otto decided that it might be best to lay low for a while and discontinue the clandestine, nightly meetings until he figured out what to do next.

Hrrmmph, he thought, lounging on his bunk one rainy afternoon in late April. *Maybe it would be best if I did leave the camp. Start over...somewhere. But how?* Escape, it seemed, was out of the question. He knew that during the last four years since thousands upon thousands of German prisoners of war held captive on American soil that only twenty or so of them had managed to escape. All, save one, had been recaptured within days – some in just a few hours – of breaking out of camp. *Here, in this small complex...with such a large hospital...and lax guards...maybe I could do it, too. And succeed. But how?* Wiping his runny nose with the sleeve of his blue woolen shirt, he snorted and closed his eyes for a nap before supper, dreaming of the possibilities.

Two days later, Otto was mopping the floor of one of the three burn units when a patient asked for water. He tried to explain in what rudimentary English he had learned during his three years a prisoner of war that it wasn't his job – or his place – to fetch and carry water for "the enemy".

"*Gott verdammt!*" the soldier retorted in perfect German. "God damn it, man! I am not your enemy. I am a prisoner, just like yourself. Just not one of war..."

Otto was taken aback. He moved closer to the patient's bed.

"*Sie deutsch*?? But not a prisoner of war?"

"*Nein*. Of course I am not a German. I just learned your language a long time ago in college. It came in handy while fighting overseas...until I was caught stealing from an officer..."

"A capital offense in any army," Otto squinted. An idea was formulating in his mind. "What did you steal?"

"Does it really matter? I was found with the goods, court-martialed, and sent to a military prison for what they thought would be a few years. But then after a few months...Hah! I escaped."

A widower for three years, with a nineteen-year-old son serving in the Navy somewhere in the South Pacific, James "Jimmy" Watts had just turned forty when he was drafted into the U.S. Army in early 1944. Like the *Wehrmacht*, the American armed forces became lax in their recruitment requirements and took just about every available man – young or older, even married men with children as well as widowers – to fill the ranks.

Landing on Omaha Beach during the D-Day invasion, Watts and what was left of his regiment fought their way to the outskirts of Paris where they met German resistance. His right shin had been shot through by a Lüger bullet, earning him an early ticket home.

"Was nearly captured myself," he chuckled, "but, see? I'm wily and wiry. Limping and bleeding, I slipped behind the lines, hid in some bushes, barked an order in German to turn those dirty, murdering Krauts away from our unit. Then, when their backs were turned, shot 'em all dead."

Otto stepped back, appalled. He tried to fight his anger, swallowing the acrid bile rising in his throat. This man – the enemy – lying in front of him...*How dare he laugh about the brutal killing of* Meine Landsleute, *my fellow countrymen? My fellow, loyal Nazis...*

"Hey, I did what I could to protect myself," Watts said in perfect German, watching Otto clench his fists. "You would have, too...if you were in my situation. But you were here, safe and sound while I was…"

"Not by choice," Otto smirked. *But if I was there,* he thought, *I wouldn't have fallen for your trick. Oldest one in the book…*

"Say…how's about that water? I'm parched. I can't reach it on the table there…""

Otto reluctantly poured a glass from the stainless steel pitcher and handed it to Jimmy. As the patient sat up, he noticed the brown-stained white bandages wrapped around his shoulders and down his left arm. Jimmy slurped a long draught and smacked his lips.

"Got this running through a barn fire," he said, following Otto's stare, "while trying to escape. 'Cause I'm still in this man's army, they sent me here for treatment before taking me to Leavenworth. That's what they think, anyway, but I ain't going! I aim to escape."

Albeit its age and nearly obsolescence, no one had been able to successfully escape from the high-security prison built in the early 1860s on the border between western Pennsylvania and southern New York to house Confederate prisoners of war.

Until Watts. It took him five nights to widen a shower drain big enough for him to slip down and dig his way through to the large sewage tunnels. On the sixth night, he followed them to a storm culvert outside the prison walls. He managed to stay on the lam for a week, stealing food and clothes when he could from garbage cans and clotheslines, sleeping under bushes and in barns.

The back of his shoulders and the upper part of his left arm were badly burned when a hay loft where he was sleeping caught fire from the embers of his cigarette. As he shimmied down the wooden ladder he was met by the owner of the farm and the local sheriff pointing a cocked snub-nosed shotgun at him. He was returned to the old Army prison and then sent to VFGH for treatment and recovery before being transported to the military prison at Fort Leavenworth, Kansas.

What Watts' crime was after he returned from France that put him in prison, Otto did not want to know. Nor did he care. He was just interested in capitalizing on Jimmy's experience and daring. *This man*, he thought, *is my one-way ticket out of here.*

"We have a lot in common," Otto said, changing

his tune of hatred to one of conciliation. "We both want to escape, don't we?"

Jimmy's eyes lit up. "Sure do…"

"When are they coming for you?"

"In a week, I think. The doctors say I am healing well enough to be able to travel soon…" He nodded thoughtfully as Otto began to sketch out a rough subterfuge.

"If one of us tries to escape, we'd be caught. No one would suspect two of us…Besides, there is a maze of tunnels under the hospital that connects all the buildings. They are used during the day, but….at night…I know how to navigate them…and you know this country. You are an American. You speak English."

In the days that followed, Otto mopped the floors and scrubbed the toilets in the burn units until they gleamed. Never had he cleaned anything so thoroughly in his life. Never had he cared so much. During his breaks and lunch, he and Jimmy hatched their plans.

Otto, Franz noticed, had not had any need for his translation skills in the last week or so.

"That is so unlike him," he whispered to Manheim one evening during supper. The camp cooks had, as usual, outdone themselves, whipping up creamy mashed potatoes to serve with the roasted pork loin and fresh, early spring green vegetables grown in the hospital "Victory" garden, now tended by some of the prisoners as part of their work. "Used to be, not a day went by when he didn't have something to complain about to the Camp Commander. Now, when I ask him if he needs me to translate, he says *nein*...he has nothing to say. And, I haven't seen him around much, either..."

"He's seldom in our barracks...Except to sleep."

"Did you ask him...?"

"No, I hardly know him. Besides, it is not my job to keep tabs on a fellow officer...If you could call him that..."

"I think he's up to something..."

"What? Our Otto?" Manheim chuckled sarcastically, slathering a scoop of butter onto his steamed broccoli and then spritzing it with juice from a lemon wedge. "Why would you ever think that?"

FIFTEEN

Two nights before Jimmy was to be discharged and taken to Leavenworth, most of the prisoners and a few ambulatory patients were crammed into the apse of the small chapel to listen to selections of "modern" jazz performed by the camp's small dance band.

Unteroffizier Otto's request to not have any "formal Christian" worship services held for the prisoners "lest they undermine our National Socialistic beliefs and ideologies" had not been honored by both the Chief Medical Officer and the prisoner of war Camp Commander. The squat brick building with its short, white silver-painted steeple, once only used as a meeting place and the occasional concert hall, was now filled with hymnals, missals, church clothes, and Scriptural tracts printed in German. A large, thick Bible graced the top of the lectern the reverend used as his pulpit.

Well, let them honor this, Otto thought as he excused himself from the rest of the officers who had gathered to attend the music fest. He then clandestinely snuck into Barracks 2 to "commandeer" another PW officer's uniform which he had earlier re-conned as Jimmy's size. Watts was so tall and skinny, it was hard to find just the right fit. It took Otto three times rummaging through closets and foot lockers until he finally found the spare uniform of lanky Dr. Kraus. It was rare these days, even during impoverished war time and the constraints of being a prisoner of war on foreign soil, to find a German so skinny.

He laughed as he returned to his own barracks. He stuffed the jackets, shirts, shoes, socks, pants, underwear, and overcoats into a large rucksack he had also "commandeered" from one of the blind patients on an ophthalmology ward. He had to wait until that young, nosy, pro-American translator, Franz Weberhardt, had taken his requisite fifteen-minute break to snag the bag.

Early the next morning, he and the other prisoners gathered to march under guard out of the stockade to their various work details. Otto was dressed as usual in his heavily soiled PW uniform. In his front pants pocket were fifty dollars in American currency that he had amassed in various, nefarious ways during his tenure as a prisoner of war. He called it his "get out of jail" money, recalling how one guard at Camp Crossline in Tennessee had tried to teach him the "all-American" game of Monopoly.

When questioned by Lieutenant Quisling about the rucksack now slung over his shoulders Otto just shrugged and nodded to Franz marching behind him to translate for him, although he knew perfectly well what the unkind MP was asking. His time with Jimmy was paying off, as he began learning a few more English words from him. Otto was just stalling for time to come up with a reasonable explanation that would satisfy the skeptical guard.

"*Ein Wechsel der Kleidung,*" he mumbled.

"*Ein* what?!" Quisling demanded, signaling for the two columns of prisoners to halt while he interrogated the *Unteroffizier.*

"A change of clothes," Franz frowned. He had a sneaky suspicion he knew what Otto was up to.

"For what? Why?"

"*Für was? Warum?*"

"*Ich habe ein Treffen mit Captain Templeton am Nachmittag. Wie Sie sehen können, ist meine Arbeit einheitlich ist verschmutzt. Ich möchte mich sauber und vorzeigbar..."*

"I have a meeting with Captain Templeton this afternoon. As you can see, my work uniform is soiled. I want to look clean...presentable..."

As the "official" camp translator, Franz wondered for a just a brief moment why he had not been told of the meeting. *Yes, Otto was definitely going to...What? Escape?* He was about to rat out Staff Sergeant Herr Otto Kempf when he suddenly recalled the minister's sermon that past Saturday.

"What would Luther have done?" Reverend Fromüeller had asked the now small, but growing cadre of prisoners who were starting to defy Otto's edict not to attend services. "Luther would have asked himself, 'What would Jesus do?' He based all of his most important decisions upon the answer."

The reverend's words had stuck home. Franz decided he would not, could not betray a fellow prisoner, even if Otto was a cruel, dishonest scoundrel about to break the law.

A moment later, Quisling jabbed the blunt end of the handle of his riding crop into Kempf's chest.

"Harrumph. I guess that's okay. It's about time you started taking care of your appearance, you slovenly, dirty Kraut!" the lieutenant scoffed at Otto's filthy uniform. He signaled for the two columns to continue marching. "Forward...Hut!"

"*Hrrumph. Ich denke, das ist okay,*" Franz said to Otto. He refrained from translating the rest of Quisling's insults. *Wait until I tell Manheim,* he thought, knowing how relieved he, like himself, would be to finally be rid of the pro-Nazi who had done everything in his power to denigrate their camp conditions. "You are very lucky," he added in German. "*Glücklich.* I hope you get away with it."

Otto sighed with relief, wiping his nose with the side of a finger. "If you tell anyone," he whispered, "I promise I will come back and kill you." Then he hoisted the rucksack fill of his and Dr. Kraus' stolen clothes and smartly marched forward.

Less than an hour later, Otto boldly rolled his new cohort sitting on the rucksack in a wheelchair swaddled in a hospital gown and two army blankets out of the burn ward on the pretext of taking him for X-rays. The doctor and two nurses on duty were so busy with other patients, they barely noticed – one even absentmindedly nodded her consent – as the two of them left. Otto hastened them through a maze of corridors to an elevator that went down to the underground tunnels.

Normally busy during the day, especially during inclement weather, on this balmy, unusually warm late April morning the tunnels were relatively empty. When an occasional nurse or doctor scurried past, Otto nodded at Jimmy, feigning sleep, "To get zee tests," he uttered, smugly sure of himself and his plan.

At the end of the last twisting tunnel was a large air vent that led up to a grate just outside the back of the prisoner stockade. Otto stopped and told Jimmy to put on Dr. Kraus' PW uniform and put the hospital gown and blankets into the rucksack. They might, he reasoned, come in handy later.

When they climbed up the narrow iron rung ladder and struggled to open the vent's grate, they found themselves standing in front of a large school bus guarded by two U.S. Army MPs. A small work detail of PWs were boarding it to be driven to the war veterans cemetery in Valley Forge State Park. Otto had heard about the detail a week earlier and volunteered himself and "a fellow prisoner" to help with the landscaping – removing dead leaves and overgrown weeds from the graves, mowing the grass, and planting new flowers. The bus driver, Otto observed, an older woman from a local limousine company, was obviously oblivious to whom her passengers were.

"I could care less," she told one of the guards. "My job is just to drive. Best not to ask any questions."

Otto and Jimmy bowed their heads and quietly got on the bus, hoping not to be recognized. So as not to be noticed, they sat in the back in deference to Jimmy's darker tinted skin. Otto's main concern, besides trying again to have to explain the rucksack they were carrying, was being recognized by either Quisling or Sergeant Cooper. But, to his great relief, a new guard, Jack Knapp, was standing in the front of their bus, a machine gun absentmindedly slung over his shoulder.

Jimmy tried to sit quietly beside Otto, but nervously scratched his stomach.

"Stop that," Otto whispered. "You don't want to draw attention to ourselves"

"Damn uniform is awful itchy. What's it made

of? Sandpaper?'

"You back there," Knapp snapped from the front of the bus. "Quit talking."

Jimmy sat on his hands to keep from scratching, but he couldn't keep from occasionally squirming. Trying to casually act like nothing else was amiss, the two prisoners rode the bus to the park and joined the others as they cleaned up the graves.

"I thought you were scrubbing toilets in the hospital," a private from Rommel's *Afrika Korps* sneered as he pushed a lawn mower past Otto. "What brings you down to cleaning graves?"

"None of your business, Heinrich," Otto sneered back. "Just a temporary change of pace for me. As *Unteroffizier,* I want to know the conditions under which all of my fellow prisoners work."

"Yeah, right. Anything to get out of harder work, eh, *Unteroffizier?* Or are you becoming, shall we say, a *model* prisoner?"

"*Halt Deinen Mund!, halte Deine Klappe*! Private Heinrich! Shut up! Or I'll put you on report!"

""*Ja, natürlich*, my Herr!" Heinrich gave Otto a smart "*Heil Hitler*" salute, stabbing his right hand and arm into the air and slapping his chest hard with his left. "I see nothing, hear nothing, say nothing."

"You'd better not. Get back to work."

Jimmy stayed close to Otto as they toiled, patiently waiting for their chance.

Right after lunch, when the two guards were out of sight – "probably napping behind the bushes or a large gravestone," he had snickered – Otto lightly tapped his partner on the shoulder and pointed to the dense woods behind the cemetery.

Too busy with finishing their own work, the other prisoners – as well as the two sleepy-eyed guards – did not notice until it was time to board the bus that evening that Otto and Jimmy had quietly slipped away.

Later that afternoon, Franz made it a point to ask Captain Templeton what time the meeting was with him and Staff Sergeant *Unteroffizier* Herr Otto Kempf. He had assumed he would be needed to translate.

"What meeting, Weberhardt?" the captain asked, concerned that he might have forgotten. "I don't think I have anything scheduled. Let me look," He thumbed through his pocket calendar, and then sighed. "No. Nothing."

""Perhaps I was mistaken. Tomorrow?"

"No. Not then either. Why do you ask?"

"*Unteroffizier* Kempf mentioned it this morning on our way from the stockade to work..." He paused, uncertain whether to betray a fellow prisoner. Even if it was Otto. Franz wondered, *If given the choice I have to make now, what would Luther do?* Closing his eyes for a brief movement in thought, he decided that the safety, as well as the morale, of the whole complex was more important than the selfish, needless escape of one of the prisoners.

"And he was carrying a rucksack containing a change of clothes..."

Warning bells rang in Captain Templeton's ears. "A change of clothes?"

"For the meeting with you...He said he wanted...for once...to look neat and tidy..."

"There is no meeting, but...Excuse me, Franz," the camp commander frowned, finally realizing what the young prisoner was trying to tell him. "I have some important business to attend to."

When Otto did not show up at the prisoner's mess that evening, Franz was certain he was no longer in the camp. He reported it to Captain Templeton the next morning.

Before *Oberfeldwebel* Otto Kempf and Corporal James Watts were officially reported missing, Captain Templeton did a thorough search of the camp, hospital grounds, and part of the surrounding countryside. After two days, when the two escapees were not found, he alerted the Phoenixville Police and then the War Department in Washington who ordered in a squadron of Military Police.

Search crews again scoured the camp, the hospital grounds, and the countryside, including the Borough of Phoenixville, the small village of Kimberton, and all of Valley Forge State Park. They then branched out to the quad-state area of Pennsylvania, New Jersey, New York, and Delaware.

But the searches proved fruitless.

Otto and Jimmy were long gone.

SIXTEEN

With Otto missing and presumed dead by most of the prisoners, the swell of pro-Nazi fervor began to ebb and finally abated. The camp atmosphere seemed lighter, now that the prisoners who did not and could not abide by the pro-Nazi idealisms felt free enough to pursue their own thoughts and feelings about being a German prisoner of war on free American soil.

They began to read the donated American novels and newspapers and discovered the joys of listening to comedic radio programs that featured such celebrated notables as Bob Hope, George Burns and Gracie Allen, Eddy Cantor, Red Skelton, and Phil Harris.

Franz's favorite evening activity as to sidle up to the radio in his own barracks and sketch while listening to *Edgar Bergen and Charlie McCarthy*, followed by the antics of American life and culture depicted in *Fibber McGee and Molly*, the droll humor of *The Life of Riley*, and Gracie Allen's uniquely creative zaniness.

Again the invitation was spread amongst them to come and worship with the Reverend Frederick Yohan Fromüeller each Saturday. Now that the *Unteroffizier* was gone along with his protestations and sanctions against any religious ceremonies, the burly pastor of Bethany Evangelical Lutheran Church was hardily and cheerfully welcomed by more and more of the prisoners. As word of his lively, humorous sermons delivered in fluent German spread throughout the camp, the chapel slowly filled to capacity. By the end of May the Lutheran services were standing room only.

A regular attendee from the very first Saturday, Franz was instantly enthralled by Pastor Freddy and his spellbinding services and rousing, often humorously entertaining sermons. He made it a point after the first service to introduce himself, Three weeks later, he asked if the reverend was available for a private chat.

Intrigued by the young prisoner who initially seemed brave enough to go against the *Unteroffizier's* wishes, Reverend Fromüeller agreed to meet Franz one weekday evening in the chapel.

"I hope you don't mind," the pastor began, "but I

made a few inquiries. Seems you are quite a talented artist..."

"*Mein Vater*...my father...he was the true artist in the family."

"Oh? And what medium did he work in? Charcoal sketches? Watercolors?"

"Oils. There are many of his paintings hanging in my mother's farmhouse..."

"Your mother's farmhouse?"

"He died before I was born. I do not know how. Mother said an illness took him. I think...the Spanish Flu?"

"*Ja*. That was rampant in the twenties after World War One. But, you say, he was the artist?" Franz nodded yes, fiddling with the large sketchpad he had brought and now held tightly on his lap. "But you've brought me some of you own work for me to look at?"

Franz nodded again.

"I did a sketch, a portrait of...Roosevelt...for the patients," he said hesitantly, "the night of the day he died. They liked it very much and now...I have an idea for another. A portrait. In oils this time...but I wanted..."

"My opinion?"

"Yes, if you don't mind."

"No. Show me."

Franz opened the sketchpad to a back page where he had drawn his study in pencil of a young man dressed in robes sitting on a bench. He was leaning against the truck of a large tree whose boughs shaded the outline of a courtyard as four doves cavorted at his feet.

"The book he is holding, see the small one? It's his *September Testament*..."

"This is of Martin Luther at Wartburg?"

"Yes, Reverend Fromüeller. I very much wish to paint him. He is a hero to me...I want to capture what he must have felt," he hesitated. "His loneliness being separated from his beloved church...his family, his friends..."

"Very much like you are feeling now. Franz?"

"Yes..."

Martin Luther, Franz once learned in Bible school, lived anonymously at the Wartburg fortress; known only as "Knight George". Leading a solitary life, the former Catholic monk began his sojourn in repose, indulging in leisure time that he had not being able, as an Augustinian, a priest, and a university professor, to enjoy in years. He wrote to a friend that he "...could not be recognized, easily taken for a soldier". With all his worldly needs attended to, he was left alone to wander freely in and around the castle and its walls, but was not allowed to go beyond them. Much of his time was spent contemplating the forests of Thuringia that encircled Wartburg below and the changing raiment of the skies above.

"Luther said," Franz explained, "that he was a 'strange prisoner...a captive with and against my own will'. That is exactly how I feel now. A prisoner of the Americans, yet a captive of my own thoughts and worries. I want to capture that in this painting of him at Wartburg."

Pastor Freddy contemplated Franz's idea.

"It is a good rendition, this sketch," Reverend Fromüeller smiled. "Perhaps putting it on canvas is helping to alleviate some of your own angst. And, perhaps, also a bit of anger?"

Franz nodded solemnly, pleased that the Lutheran minister was so easily able to read into his soul. He frowned, etching into his mind the reverend's insightful comments.

"Perhaps, it would be a metaphor for my life. A visual depiction in oils of the life and feelings of every prisoner...."

"Yes, that would be true, too. If nothing else, a remembrance of your time here so isolated from your mother...your life in Eisenach before the war.

"Please, tell me about her. And, of course, who is it...Greta?"

SEVENTEEN

Even after all those years, the one thing Gwen Weberhardt missed most about her dear husband was the scent of his cherry pipe tobacco that permeated deep into the crevices of their small farmhouse on the outskirts of Eisenach. Every evening after dinner, she reminisced, he would sit at the large hand-hewn wooden table, sketching, endlessly sketching drafts; steady wisps of smoke curling up from his Meerschaum pipe as he drew. Often he would regal her with humorous stories about his drawings that would later be transformed into the many oil paintings that now adorned the walls of her rustic farmhouse.

She had hopes back then that one day he would be a famous artist, recognized far beyond their small village for his great talent. But he claimed he was happiest farming their small homestead during the day and painting at night.

"No need to go public," he smiled as he worked, munching on a piece of her home-baked apple strudel warmed by the open fire. "We are most nearly content, my dear."

Most nearly.

Those two words greatly grieved her, knowing that his life would have been totally complete had they had a son while he was still alive. But when the fever suddenly struck and took him from her a week later, she was still not sure she was pregnant. To tell him would have raised false hopes if she wasn't; not telling him if she was meant he would die a disappointed man. In the end, just before he passed away, she whispered the news in his ear. He died a happy man.

Fifteen years later, she still lived on the farm, managing it with their young son who had inherited his father's artistic talent. A few of Franz's earlier oil paintings hung proudly on the walls next to those of her husband. And while Gunther had painted with broad, bold, colorful strokes, his son's were delicately fine, detailed with muted earth tones. Two of Gwen's favorites were of the late summer sun rising over the Hainich Mountains – one by her husband, the other by Franz – both hanging side-by-side over her bed.

A product of generations of good Teutonic

stock, she was an ample, buxom woman with deep set brown eyes and a short-cropped mop of dark blond, unruly curly hair that she kept tamed under a blue and white striped kerchief. Tall and formidable, it seemed that nothing could phase nor scare her. And hardly anything did. Yet, when the two Gestapo *offiziers* pounded on their door the morning of Franz's birthday, she was badly frightened for her and Franz's safety and that of they young girl he said he was going to meet at the castle.

That afternoon after the two of them spent exploring the fortress of Wartburg, Franz walked Greta home. They leisurely strolled the mile or so to the lane that led up to the Hornweitz's tiny stone farmhouse until they heard what they thought was thunder rumbling in the distance.

"There is a storm coming, Franz..." Greta said, a tinge of panic in her voice. "Let's hurry and get inside the house before it starts to rain."

"That is not thunder, Greta. It is too steady. Listen. It sounds more like many soldiers marching in unison...And they are coming closer." When the loud, rhythmic noise was nearly upon them, he pulled his young companion into a copse of trees.

"Here...Hide!" he whispered, motioning her to crutch low beside him.

A large contingent of SS Storm Troopers, goose-stepping to a fast-paced cadence, marched by as Franz and Greta cowered under the bushes.

"They are coming to get my and my family, I know," she whispered. Franz put a forefinger against her lips to silence her. He shook his head, and then peered through the thick, low branches. When the soldiers had passed by and he thought it safe to venture back out onto the lane, he slithered out of the copse and beckoned Greta to follow him.

"I think it's safe now...Come quickly. Let's get you home before they return. You'll be safe there. At least until..."

"My family..." Greta sobbed as she lagged behind Franz. "We are to leave early tomorrow morning. Mother is packing now...Father says we can walk to the shore..."

"Tomorrow might be too late," he said. "The Gestapo was here this morning looking for me...and for *Juden*..."

"Why didn't you tell me while we were at the castle?"

"I didn't want to frighten you. But now that those troops are in the area, you are in grave danger"

"I always was..."

Franz remembered the history of the village he had learned in school. Between the 1860s and 1938, Eisenach had hosted one of the largest Jewish communities in their province of Thuringia. They had migrated from the Rhön area near Stadtlengsfeld to Eisenach after being emancipated in the early 1800s. At the beginning of the century, there were nearly 500 members. He remembered two years ago in November 1938 when their new synagogue, built in 1885, was destroyed by the Nazis during the bloody *Kristallnacht*.

Most of the Jewish population had "disappeared" after that. Some managed to escape to other countries. Those who were brave enough to stay in the area, like Greta Hornweitz and her family, had fled into the countryside, hiding in plain sight. Others were not so lucky and were rounded up like cattle, loaded into filthy railroad box cars, and imprisoned in detention camps in Poland.

He did not want that to happen to his new

friend.

But when Franz and Greta arrived at the Hornweitz's farmhouse, it had been razed to the ground. There was no trace of her parents or of her two younger siblings.

"We must go back to my mother..." Franz said, holding Greta in his thin arms as she wailed in utter despondency.

"*Meine Liebe Eltern*..." she sobbed.

"Yes, yes, your dear parents...But they may have escaped...perhaps even have left before the storm troopers got here. We must hurry now...before they come back..."

"We must help her," Franz begged his mother after he and Greta explained that she was a non-Aryan Jew and what had happened to the Hornweitz farm. He reminded Gwen of the rumors rampant in the small village of concentration camps and large gas ovens that the Nazi propaganda machine tried to convince the populace did not really exist. Even when the many residents of whole neighborhoods disappeared overnight and never returned. "We...we can't let that happen...to Greta," he pleaded.

"We...I will try to save her," Gwen promised Fanz. With the shortage of food, she had hardly enough to feed herself and her son let alone having another one in the family, as it were, to take care of. Nonetheless, she felt it was her Christian duty.

"Now even more so." He turned to his mother, tears welding up in his eyes. "*Mutter*, what can we do? *Bitte*...Please?"

"We will give her a pair of your britches and an old chambray shirt," Gwen said. She turned to the still weeping Greta. "What else you may need, I can provide. For now, you will stay covered in hay under the altar until we, I can figure something out."

Now she feared even more for their safety should the Storm Troopers come back; not only for herself and her son, but also for the young Jewish girl now cowering in the barn under the secret altar Franz had built a few years ago in the barn stall where, at night, she housed two ewes and their four small young sheep.

For a few months after that, Gwen did her best to keep Greta hidden. Slight of build and clad in her son's cast-off clothes, with most of her sleek black hair clipped off by Gwen and capped with a knitted ski cap, Greta could easily have passed as one of Franz's younger cousins. But that, she had hoped, would not be necessary just as long as Franz faithfully attended the *Hitler Jugend* meetings and kept quiet about their guest. If he did, there would be not be any reason for the *offiziers* to come back again to find him...and to accidentally stumble upon their house guest.

As much as he hated the daily meetings and the forced marching, Franz remained outwardly faithful to *der Grund Nazi*. In the days and weeks that she had come to live with him and his mother, he had fallen in love with Greta and would do anything not to jeopardize her life. Even if it meant he had to pretend to pay homage to Adolph Hitler and his wickedly vicious thugs.

At all costs, keep your mouth shut, he constantly chided himself as he trudged the two miles into Eisenach to attend the meetings. Even if he did take an oath to "tell" the Gestapo "everything" about any suspected traitors he might know – friends or family – he pledged to himself never to tell anyone about

Greta. He keep cadence with his silent mantra: *No body must know. No body must know.*

When not in hiding, Greta pitched in to help Gwen with her daily chores. She turned out to be an able, conscientious worker, but a less than somewhat sociable companion, often giving into long periods of silence.

Franz's mother knew that the young girl was in the deep troughs of grief and was relieved when she finally started to play with the many chickens and Gwen's two Alsatian dogs, Willy and Joe, that followed Greta around the farm. That, to Franz's mother, was a good sign; both for Greta's well-being and for her trustworthiness.

"Always trust your dog," Gunther had often said. "If he likes someone, chances are, he's *Ein guter Mensch*...a good person." After many months working side-by-side with the young girl, Gwen finally came to realize long before her son did, that Greta might just make a fine wife for him.

With that in mind, she invited the young *Juden* out from under the altar in the barn and into the spare room next to the kitchen, treating Greta as if she was, in fact, Gwen's own daughter.

When Franz went that one year to the nearby University of Efburt to start his medical studies, and was later conscripted into the Army *Medical Korps* when he turned eighteen, Greta continued to remain on the farm with Gwen. There was, of course, no place else for her to go.

Before he left, Franz had promised that when he returned he would marry Greta and keep her safe from harm forever. And so she stayed on and helped her future mother-in-law, posing when necessary to be her orphaned nephew.

And, for a little more than two years, as long as they managed to provide the allotted share of their farm goods to the *Wehrmacht* every other month or so they had gotten away with their ruse. The weary German soldiers who came for the supplies were just as deceived as Gwen's small cadre of friends and their neighbors. Most of them, even if they did recognize Greta dressed up in Franz's out-grown britches and shirts, as the "young Jewish Hornweitz girl gone missing," had turned a blind eye.

Yet, the threat of being discovered harboring a *Junge jüdische Mädchen*, hung over Gwen. *What if a friend is really a spy? What if a neighbor betrayed me?*

she often thought. Hiding *Juden* was a serious crime that meant deportation along with Greta to a death camp and most certainly being annihilated. Despite her occasional black thoughts, Gwen tried to remain optimistic, maintaining her fearless illusion that everything seemed to be going rather well. If not for her own sake, but for that of the young girl. And for her son.

After all, she reasoned, *we've been safe under the shadow of Wartburg for this long. Why would it not continue for yet a while longer?*

Then a letter from America, post-dated three months ago, was delivered by hand by an older gentleman claiming to be a "representative from the Swedish Red Cross". Franz wrote that he was now a prisoner of war, held captive somewhere in a strange place called Texas.

EIGHTEEN

"Their letters – my mother would put both hers and Greta's into one envelope – stopped coming a year or so ago," Franz told Reverend Fromüeller. "While I was still in Camp Texia. I kept on faithfully sending mine, though. Our allotment of two letters and a postcard a week. With each one, I'd hope and pray that I would hear back from them...but...*Nein.* Nada. Nothing."

Pastor Freddy squinted, knitting his thick brown eyebrows together. "Hmm..." he thought out loud. "I am a member of the Lutheran Commission for Prisoners of War. They often communicate with the International Red Cross, as well as their Swedish liaisons to Germany. Let me see if they can't help find out about your mother. And Greta..."

"For whatever you can do," Franz whispered. "I will be *Ewig dankbar.* Eternally grateful.

"I cannot promise anything. From what you tell me, and what I hear and read about what is going on in your country, there may not be any, er, hope. But, still...

"Like Luther would do, we must put our faith…and fate…in the hands of God."

"I will try to do that, Pastor Freddy. "But…"

"Sssh…We don't know anything for sure and won't until we try. *Ja?*"

"*Ja.*"

Whatever the outcome of his efforts, Franz already had in mind how he would thank the Reverend Fromüeller.

NINETEEN

Happy once again to be able to actively and freely partake in Lutheran services, and reveling in his new, budding friendship with Pastor Freddy, Franz quickly lost interest in wondering to where Otto and the lanky burn patient might have disappeared. Instead, he concentrated on renewing his faith, honing his art, and assiduously performing his duties on the ophthalmology wards.

He harbored hope in his mind and in his heart beside his homesickness for Eisenach, his mother, and his loneliness for Greta that the reverend and the commission might just be able to find them. Franz prayed night and day for their safety.

And as he continued to work on the new portrait, he realized that he was also beginning to again feel good about his life.

TWENTY

In mid-March, a letter signed by all the members of the local American Legion Post had appeared on the Op Ed page of *The Daily Republican* publically denouncing the presence of any and all German prisoners of war housed "and otherwise maintained and/or working" in the area and called for their "immediate removal and departure" from the Valley Forge General Hospital.

On April 13, an article appeared stating that due to national public outcry over the prisoners receiving the same, if not better food than the patients, as well as eating "better" than the American public who had "…sacrificed so much…including suffering sub-standard food," the rations of those encamped in the Valley Forge General Hospital complex would be "…substantially cut down and limited" to match the rations of the patients and the average American family.

Two days later, Evie G. Radnor, one of the borough's older leading and most influential socialites who had lost her son in the Battle of the

Ardenne, wrote a letter to the editor stating that allowing prisoners of war to "directly attend to our brave wounded...is putting our honored soldiers in the gravest of danger and is a disgrace to the memory of those who fought so valiantly and died while defending our American freedoms."

She also sent a signed carbon copy to Colonel Beakers via private messenger, noting in the margin that it was his "responsibility to do something about this. Immediately!"

The morning paper was opened on Suzanne's desk at work to the editorial page on which Evie's letter appeared. She read the articles and the letter with avid interest while munching on a luncheon sandwich made with minced sausages leftover from last night's dinner.

"Why would German medical personnel" – she refrained from calling them "prisoners" – "do anything to harm our boys?" she wondered out loud. "After all, they are prisoners and closely guarded." Her father had carefully, and gently, explained to the family just a few days ago, when Rose Ann and her mother had expressed fears of being raped in town by an "escaped con German bully," that even though they were prisoners of war, none of them at the hospital were hostile in any way. There were no reports of them harming any of the patients.

"Rest assured, my dears, none of them are even allowed off the base," he smiled. "And they have been nothing but cooperative as they work around the hospital, taking very good care of our men." While he knew of the "incident" involving the death of the German doctor, he refrained from mentioning it. All of the hospital staff and maintenance personnel were politely, but firmly asked by Colonel Beakers not to say anything about it to anyone outside of the hospital complex.

"What they don't know won't hurt them," the Post Commander stated during a staff meeting, citing the old trite adage. "More importantly, what they don't know won't frightened them..."

"Lots of people in town are afraid of them," John said, standing behind Suzanne and peering over her shoulder. "I know Mrs. Radnor quite well. Used to mow her lawn when I was a kid. She was tense and edgy back then, and when the war came and she lost Christopher...Well, she's just frightened. And I can't say that I blame her."

"But they are under guard...and my father says –
he works there – sees them every day...And nothing
bad has happened."

"Nothing that he isn't telling you. Maybe that is
so, but he doesn't know them like I do." He paused,
deciding what to say next. "Over there...I saw...Some
of them are cruel, unfeeling, uncaring...The atrocities
I've heard about...They are capable of anything."

"Even harming our boys while they are
prisoners?"

"Even then...I wouldn't put it past any of them."

Suzanne shuttered at the thought. She was sure
John was right, He probably did know more about
the Germans – he still collectively called them "the
enemy" – than her father. *But surely, if Poppa says
there is nothing to worry about...That we are safe,
then..."*

"Say, I was thinking," John said, interrupting her
thoughts. "I've been stopping by here during work to
see you for the past three months or so...Don't you
think it's about time we, um...well..."

Suzanne felt her cheeks flush and the small knot
that fluttered in her chest each time she even saw,

let alone chat with him, tighten. She had been hoping for this moment, when he would finally have the courage to ask her out. But it seemed this time would be like all the other times when he had begun to broach the subject. *He's going to back down. Again.* She sighed inwardly.

"Yes, John?" she asked, looking up at him expectantly. Perhaps she should be the one to...No, that would be unseemly. She recalled her mother telling her time and time again that a woman's place was to be submissive...To let the man take the lead...

"Well...Susie...er, Suzanne. I was thinking..."

"About...What?" she asked rather coyly. *Get on with it, John...Please! I can't bear to wait any longer.*

"Well, now that I have this job...and all...Well, I've been saving a bit of money and I found this kinda beat up car. Well, not so beat up. It's a 1935 – pre-war and all. Not a Flickr, although I've always wanted one, but they're too expensive. But, anyway...It's a 1935 Ford Roadster. You know...a top 'em down car. Two-seater, with a rumble in the back, over the trunk. I plan on cleaning it up on Saturday and then, maybe, after that...that evening we could..."

"Suzanne!" Uncle Charlie called, barreling through the reception area and into her small office. "I need copies of last week's orders. Damn foreman seems to have lost the list and one of them was screwed up. We need to order more of those blasted gas carburetors and I need to figure out from whom. Dang war...Oh!" He stopped mid-stride in the door frame when he saw John Voight talking with his ace assistant bookkeeper. "Whoops! Sorry. Didn't mean to interrupt, but, Suzanne..."

"Yes, Uncle Charlie. I'll get right on it. Do you want one copy or two?"

"Two, yes, two would be fine...If that's okay."

"No problem. I gather you know John Voight, our new shipping clerk..."

"Actually, assistant manager," John said, smiled shyly "I was promoted a few days ago. Just forgot to tell you..."

"Forgot to tell me?" Suzanne bristled. "Since when..."

"Say, son, how are you getting on here?" her uncle asked. "Everything to your liking?" He glanced at the young couple, sensing the taut equanimity between them. Much more than that of a mere relationship between co-workers. He smiled. "Work-wise, I mean."

"Oh, yes...Yes, sir," John smiled back, trying very hard not to keep his eyes on Suzanne. "Very well, indeed, sir. No complaints. Work-wise, that is."

"Well, that's just fine. Just dandy. Now that I've given Suzanne a bit of work to do..." Charles Kessler nodded at the remains of Suzanne's sandwich and half-eaten apple on her desk, "...after lunch...I've a bit of an inventory problem that I know only you can solve, Mr. Voight. If you can tear yourself away..."

"Yes, Mr. Kessler. Right away. Sir."

"Um, yes. Now would be most convenient..." Uncle Charlie stood sideways against the door jamb, ready to usher John out.

"Well, I, um..." John looked down at Suzanne. He frowned at the exasperating look on her face.

Not again! Thanks, Uncle Charlie, she thought sarcastically, as she watched the young ex-Army turret gunner walk slowly away from her desk toward her Uncle Charlie.

Please...John...Johnny...Before you leave, just say...something!

"Sure, Mister Kessler. I'm coming. Right now."

He stopped mid-stride and turned back to Suzanne, about to angrily bite into the rest of her apple. "How about I pick you up…Saturday?" he blurted out." Late Saturday afternoon? Around four-thirty? In my new, old Ford Roadster?"

"Come on, son," Uncle Charlie said. "Time's a' wasting. There's still a war on, you know."

"That would be fine, John," Suzanne said emphatically, putting the half-eaten apple down. "I look forward to it." Blushing under her uncle's knowing smile – he winked and gave her a thumbs up as they left – she lowered her eyes and began to clear the newspaper and the remaining fragments of lunch from her desk.

Finally! He asked. And I…

I said, "YES!!"

Twenty-One

That night, after the family listened to an episode of *The Jack Benny Program* in their upstairs sitting room, Suzanne asked her father about Mrs. Radnor and her letter. And, once again, she questioned him about how safe the borough really was with so many prisoners housed close by.

"Only two hundred and forty or so now that..." Abram Kessler stopped, afraid once again to mention the brutal death of the elderly German physician in the dark of night and the all too coincidental resultant disappearance of a prisoner of war and a patient from one of the burn wards the following week. "Ahem. Well, despite Mrs. Radnor's alarming comments...We're all safe."

"But John said..."

"Johnny Voight may know about Germans in general. But I know in particular about the Germans imprisoned at the hospital. They are two different animals..."

"Animals, Poppa!?!" Rose Ann exclaimed. She crawled onto the brocade covered settee next to her mother's assurance and comfort against the unknown. "Wild animals?! Oh, please! Say it isn't so!"

"That's not what I meant," Abram tried to explain. "The prisoners are not, by any means, 'animals'. That is only a figure of speech. An analogous comparison." His voice softened. "I am sure that eventually, eventually...Colonel Beakers and Captain Templeton will make the right decision when it comes to the safety of the patients, the residents of Phoenixville...and the prisoners. Trust in that. Believe me."

He wearily rose and retired to the sanctuary of his and Katrina's master bedroom, suddenly tired and overly burdened by the now quarrelsome dilemma of foreign aliens incarcerated on familiar ground.

TWENTY-TWO

A little less than a month later, on Tuesday, May 8, 1945, the Allied victory over Germany was declared.

Suzanne and John were sharing lunch at a wooden picnic table on a side lawn of Kessler and Gulden when an announcement came over the company loudspeakers: "We won the war!" her Uncle Charlie exclaimed. "Hitler is dead. Germany has surrendered!" To celebrate, he stated that the plant was hereby closed for the rest of the day.

In the weeks that followed, newspapers and magazines were flooded with reports and pictures of thousands of emaciated Jewish people being liberated from the concentration camps strewn across northern Europe. The majority of Phoenixville, as well as the rest of the country, were in total disbelief. To Suzanne, the horrific stories were further proof that what John had said about German atrocities were true.

And then there was yet again another article in *The Daily Republican* alluding to pro-Nazi German citizens and prisoners of war, angry that the war was lost, retaliating with violence against their captors. With her father working so close to and with PWs at the Army hospital, she began to fear for his life.

Franz cheered out loud when he heard the news that the war was finally over. It meant he would soon be able to go home again; albeit probably a war-torn home. But still...He was anxious to find out what had happened to his mother and to Greta. He had read the reports of the many German concentration camps and was distraught and dismayed that that might be the fate of his dear *Mutter* and young *Fraulein.*

Der liebe Got, he prayed. *Bitte. Ich hoffe, es wird nicht so sein. Dear God. Please. I hope it will not be so.*

Each evening after work, he went to the Prisoners' Commissary to peer at the disturbingly graphic pictures in the American newspapers and magazines and scan the lists of emancipated prisoners hoping to find Gwen and Greta's faces and names.

He became even more despondent when Pastor

Freddy's dauntless efforts to obtain information about his mother and sister through both the Lutheran Commission and the International Red Cross had so far come up empty. There was no record of a "Greta Hornweitz" or even a "Greta Weberhardt" anywhere in all of Germany. His mother, the IRC reported after requesting a search in Eisenach, had not been seen, according to one of their neighbors, on the Weberhardt farm since late 1943, a scant year and a half after Franz had gone to war and had subsequently been captured.

While he feared the worst, he still harbored a faint hope that they, at least his mother, would still be alive.

"I tried," the Reverend Fromüeller said. "I am so sorry I can't bring you better news. But, we can hope. And pray."

"Yes, yes. *Danke schön*. I appreciate it," Franz nodded. "But you've done all you can do. Now it's up to me to find them if...when I return home."

TWENTY-THREE

Toward the end of that mild summer of 1945, after much hemming and hawing and vehement protestations from Captain Templeton, who had sworn up and down many more times then both of them could count, that none of the prisoners were a threat, Colonel Beakers reluctantly ordered that the prisoners were to cease all "...viable work that involved close contact with our American solders..."

"They are not all pro-Nazis..." Templeton averred. "In fact, most of them, now that the war is officially over, want to stay and become American citizens..."

"Regardless," the colonel stated. "Most of them are to be reassigned to more menial chores around the campus." In a staff memo as well as in a statement released to *The Daily Republican* and also printed in *The Forge*, the weekly hospital newsletter, he reasoned that his decision was to prevent "...further incurrence of the wrath of the local citizenry...and to maintain the status quo and high morale in and of the current hospital staff..." He was quite adamant that the prisoners immediately begin service in more "menial, but quite necessary tasks…"

"And we certainly can't take the chance of fostering any further animosity from Phoenixville residents toward the hospital and our noble colleagues. It's the best solution for all of us," he winced. "At least for now."

Colonel Beakers had admitted in February that the addition of the 250 or so prisoners with "…vast medical experience on and off the field of battle…aiding in and around the hospital with care of our patients was a welcomed boon," had greatly helped to ease the stress of the then overworked skeletal American staff. But with his edict, there would once again be a dire lack of adequate medical personnel in the wards. Not one to pander to his troops, he solemnly, and reluctantly, urged his hospital staff, with its lack of sufficient manpower, to "make the best of it…"

Within a few days, the prisoners – doctors, surgeons, medics, and orderlies alike – were reassigned to other areas around the hospital grounds as far away as possible from any further contact with the wounded of their former "enemy".

Consequently, quite capable and very able-bodied medical professionals, albeit Germans, were now tediously doing boring, unskilled tasks as needed: swabbing floors, scrubbing toilets and cleaning latrines just as *Unteroffizier* Herr Otto "the Medic" Kempf had done before his great escape.

Like prisoners in more than 500 other camps across the country, they joined the ranks of general laborers, planting and maintaining vegetable gardens, doing minor electrical and construction work, working in the five hospital laundry rooms scattered under the buildings, accessed only by the maze of tunnels. A few learned to cook, while others helped the hospital carpenters, tailors, laundry staff, and automotive mechanics.

"Anything," Beaker said much to his own angry disappointment, "to keep them away from our patients...But, there is no use in riling up the residents...Who really don't know...don't understand what we are really trying to do here."

Franz, to his initial great disappointment and sad chagrin, found himself also doing menial tasks. After much deliberation by Captain Templeton, who had been told of Franz's assiduousness and had come to admire the many drawings the young prisoner had already done of the camp and its surroundings as well as the charcoal portrait of FDR now framed and hanging in the ophthalmology ward, assigned him to assist Abram Kessler in the engineering department. There Franz was put to work cleaning the boilers and furnaces, carrying ashes to the slag heap at the very back of the hospital grounds and toting coal back from the huge piles housed in a large brick warehouse in the back of the complex, next to the stockade. These were not tasks, he decided, conducive to his gaining more medical knowledge. Nor were they really a welcomed adjunct to his artistic nature.

Look on the bright side, he continuously tried to tell himself and later said to the reverend.

"Besides," as you once asked. "What would Luther have done?"

"Make the best of it!" Pastor Freddy said enthusiastically.

"Yes, and if nothing else, I can garner free bits and pieces of hard bituminous coal to sketch with, without having to buy soft drawing pencils at the commissary."

"So, you with your hard-earned eighty cents a day prisoner's script saved, you can use it for something, um, more worthwhile. Not that drawing pencils are not..."

"I know, Reverend Fromüeller. To most my art supplies are just trivialities. But to me, they are...my life." He paused. "But, I suppose you are right. I will need the money when I finally return home to Eisenach."

But these thoughts and speculations, however, were very little comfort to him.

And while *Herr*...Mister Kessler was overly friendly toward him as he directed their work, Franz was more than mildly disgruntled.

Banned from the hospital wards, there was no way of finding out about all those he had come to know and to care for, despite persistently asking Captain Templeton and, now, Mr. Kessler. They both refused to tell him anything.

When he bitterly complained to the minister, he was told the same thing.

"Sorry, son. But any discussion about the patients now is *Strengstens verboten*. Strictly forbidden."

He missed the patients to whom he had tended. He wondered what would, had happened to Tom, the young Merchant marine, who had "oohed" and "ahhed" at the descriptions of his sketches of the camp and its occupants. He wondered about the older infantryman whose facial burns were so severe and painful that not even heavy doses of morphine would help. He recalled when the corporal grabbed his hand and asked to be helped to end his life.

"I am no good like this...looking like this...not being able to see...Please help me...end it all..."

But Franz could not, would not. And did not.

"It is not right," he had said in English, at first not realizing until afterward the lame, inappropriate pun. "Somehow, God will see you through..."

He calmly sat by the patient's side whispering stories of his native Eisenach while the nearly blind soldier drifted of to sleep. It was the last time Franz had been able to be with him.

Suddenly shrouded in silence, except for the occasional meaningless chats with his bunkmates and the rare visits with Manheim, he spent what little free time he now had by himself listening to news and comedy shows on the radio, reading, and assiduously working on the painting.

Manheim, he sadly thought as he applied a light tan wash to the canvas for the castle walls in the background, was assigned to work on one of the carpentry crews, shoring up the walls of the new gymnasium. He would eventually help to mix and pour cement for the new Olympic-sized swimming pool being built for patient therapy sessions. Franz thought this was truly unfair; a total waste of the bone setter's time and talents.

He did not know why he and the others were reduced to such menial tasks and circumstances. No one on the hospital staff, not even Captain Templeton, had thought to explain to the prisoners why they were torn from their originally assigned tasks and were now being treated like slaves. Young, talented, and now lonely Franz Weberhardt felt utterly lost and betrayed.

Very much like Martin Luther probably was, he surmised. *I feel so much like him now in 1945 that he must have felt in 1521. How can I possibly portray that in my painting of him?*

That night, he prayed for guidance.

Perhaps, the answer came just as he was about to drift off into sleep, *Pastor Freddy, the burly, but kind and gentle, Lutheran minister, might be able to* help.

TWENTY-FOUR

They quickly scrambled through the dense woods and down a ravine edged by the shiny tracks of the Pennsylvania Railroad along the portion of the Schuylkill River that ran through the park.

"We're in luck!" Jimmy excitedly exclaimed, knocking his knuckles against a rail as if to call upon the gods of good fortune. "If we wait long enough, a freight train is bound to lumber by...and then we can hop a box...and we are on our way!" He laughed and slapped Otto's shoulder.

"'Hop a box'? What is that?"

"Don't you know? Hop on a box car. Ride the rails. Bum a ride. Don't you Krauts do that in Germany? Why, we can go all the way west, I bet," Jimmy explained. "A free ride to freedom, my friend. The railroad, just like back in the olden days...when my people...Well, that was a different kind of railroad...but, just the same. On the way to freedom!"

"What are you talking about?" Otto said, looking around to make sure they weren't discovered hiding under the bracken and yew bushes along the tracks.

The more he learned about his now new travelling companion, the more he realized he did not know. "Never mind. You can tell me later. Just shut up and let me think."

They waited in the underbrush in silence until, an hour later, a long freight train slowly crawled by as it navigated the sharp curve.

"Come on!" Jimmy cried as he ran to catch a hand rail on one of the box cars. Its sliding door was open to the near dark and semi-emptiness within. "Now's our chance. Follow me!"

He easily grabbed hold, swung his long, lean body onto the straw-strewn wooden floor and reached down to help Otto running alongside.

"That's it, grab the rail...now grab my arm. Keep running and on the count of...TWO! Jump up. There. I've got you," Jimmy smiled when Otto flopped panting alongside him. "Easy as pun'kin pie!"

The box car was half filled with crates. Otto looked out the open door, squinted in the setting sun, ascertaining that they were, in fact, heading west. Where west, they did not know. But by the looks of the labels on the crates, they would not starve while on the journey.

For more days than Otto could later count, they slept on thin layers of prickly straw, taking turns using the stuffed rucksack for a pillow. A few chiggers and lice invaded their now soiled uniforms, but Otto managed to pop them dead with his fingernails, telling Jimmy as he did lewd and bawdy jokes in German. Jimmy frowned at his companion's crassness, but laughed politely anyway. But they ate, as Jimmy said, "in style", eating their way through a variety of goods packed in tin and glass containers all opened with Jimmy's Swiss Army knife.

"I've concealed it all dis time...in my underwear. No one ever found it," he said. "Nobody ever thought to look..."

They dined on cold or, at best, lukewarm, canned corn; green beans; tinned meats, including Spam, cocktail wieners and deviled ham; creamed spinach; sauerkraut; diced tomatoes; diced potatoes; dill pickle spears crammed in squared squat glass containers; and chucks of pear preserves fished with their grimy fingers out of wax-sealed Mason jars. When they were fully satiated, they slept.

Through the many layovers in myriad yards as the box car was shuffled around from one train consist to another they often hid in the back of the car, behind the crates. And sometimes, while the car lay idle in a yard, they jumped out at night to stretch their legs and catch a smoke; discovering and raiding two of the larger crates that contained cartons of Lucky Strikes.

Finally, they wound up in a train yard just outside Racine, Wisconsin.

Watts had turned out to be quite a talkative, well-educated braggart; full of himself, his adventures, and what he called his "varied accomplishments". Before the war, after his wife died, he was a union organizer in New Jersey; used to giving, not taking orders.

"When I got back from the war, I was stationed at Fort Dix to recuperate from my gunshot wound. They gave me a job, pushing papers around a desk. Not for me," he explained to Otto one evening as they sat smoking their purloined cigarettes, their feet dangling over the edge of the opened boxcar door. "I was used to agitating...forming unions in Northern factories. The officer in charge, he was so full of himself, his hot air could have easily floated him away. I hated him and his superior, uppity ways...bossing me around like I was nothing. He never bothered to find out what I did in civilian life, managing and overseeing a multitude of unionized workers."

"*Ja*, I can see how that could be problem," Otto said, blowing a smoke ring above his head. It was a new talent he had learned from Jimmy and was proudly showing it off, even if it was just to himself.

"Now, that one's really good. You're getting the hang of it, Mister Kempf."

"Name's Otto."

"Sure. Well, this Major kept on bossing me around, ordering me to do foolish, meaningless things. So much so, I got down-right tired of it...So, one night, I snuck back into the admin office were we worked and stole his prized German luger and this pocket knife..."

"And you got caught?"

"Not until I was bragging about it to another soldier, who turned me in...And that slip of the tongue – as they say, 'Loose lips do sink ships!' – got me court-martialed and sent to that old prison in northern Pennsylvania. Dagnabbit...I should have known better. But as you now well know, I am a cocky old man..."

"So, you escaped, got burnt...and here you are."

"Yep. Here I am. You know the rest..." Jimmy took a long pull on his cigarette and blew a large ring out of the side of his mouth. "So, Otto...What about you? Why are you so dead set against our democracy?"

"Don't start that again, Jimmy," Otto scowled. "You know how much I believe in Hitler and his ideology." He refrained from acknowledging his subsequent disappointment and bitter growing disillusionment.

"Yeah, so? What's he got our government doesn't?"

"Had. He killed himself and his wife – even his innocent dogs – in a bunker just before your troops could get to him..."

"I am truly sorry, for your sake, to hear that. But that man deserved what he got, starting a big war like he did."

"Could be," Otto admitted. He was beginning to rethink his fanatic zeal for Nazi pseudo-theology. What did it get him in the end? Capture and imprisonment by the enemy. And now he was nearly desolate, on the lam in a foreign country, with no money, no job, and no place to go. *Maybe*, he decided, *I'll listen more closely to Jimmy's tales of the fruits of American Democracy. What harm could it do?*

After a few weeks, Otto became bored riding the rails. While Jimmy was an amiable companion, he was pretty serious about his vast knowledge of American history and the inner workings of the democratic government of its United States. Otto decided it was time he learned more about the country he was disappearing into. During many a long night, Jimmy told him about the Declaration of Independence, the American Revolution and the subsequent formation of the government "for the people, by the people, and of the people...that shall not perish from this earth..."

"Hah! It almost did by German hands," Otto laughed.

"But it didn't..." Jimmy smiled. "Then came the Civil War and all that entailed...with the Negroes being freed and all...That's when the labor laws started taking effect...Let me tell you about the

Pennsylvania mines and the strikes and how unionization got started. That's the interesting part...my forte..."

By the time they had gotten to Racine, Jimmy was steadily lecturing Otto on the causes and effects of the Spanish-American War, Teddy Roosevelt carrying a big stick, why the United States entered the First World War, the misguided reasons for Prohibition and its judicious repeal, the Great Depression, and FDR's work programs.

After three nights in the rail yard, they finally realized the boxcar which they called "home" for weeks was going no further. Jimmy and Otto gathered what foodstuffs they could carry in the knapsack and their pockets and, right after dawn on the fourth day, just before a crew came to unload the boxcar, snuck around the myriad train cars and through the maze of tracks to the outskirts of town.

In the dim light of the rising sun, they stole two sets of civilian work clothes hanging to dry behind a long stretch of row homes and burned the PW uniforms in an incinerator behind a second-rate diner. They then went inside for a bit of breakfast and to ask if there was any work available.

"Say, who are you guys?" the short order cook asked from behind the counter. "Drifters?"

"We look like drifters?" Jimmy smirked, straightening the collar of the clean shirt he had just put on. "We're just two fellas fresh home from the war, looking for work. Same as all the others. I'm, er, James," he stated, realizing there wasn't any sense lying about his first name. "And this is my buddy, Otto."

"Actually, William," Otto cut him off. "William Otto. Otto William..."

"Which one is it, young man?" the cook said. "Make up your mind."

"Otto. Call me Otto," he smiled. "How do you do?" he asked, using his best English in the hopes that no one would detect his accent.

"Well...I don't know," the cook thoughtfully frowned, whipping a soiled white towel over his shoulder. "I could use some help cleaning up the joint; doing some painting...general maintenance. That kind of stuff. You interested?"

"And a place to stay?" Jimmy asked.

"Got a room with a bathroom in back..."

"We will be guards, then, too," Otto added.

"*Ja*...er, yes. We will work for you...Er, you are?"

"Frank. Name's Frank. Welcome aboard. When you've finished your eggs, I'll show you around."

Otto wasn't too pleased about scrubbing floors and toilets again. But, as Jimmy, pointed out, "a job is a job and we both need the money."

They worked for Frank for a month before they heard that the U.S. Army was diligently searching for twenty or so escaped prisoners of war who, from a few of the 511 PW camps scattered across the country, were still at large.

He reasoned it wouldn't be too long before their employer realized they weren't newly discharged American soldiers bumming their way across the country, but two of the wanted escapees.

Once again, Otto had a plan.

TWENTY-FIVE

On that bright, but chilly moonlit night. John pulled up in front of the Kessler's home, shifted into neural, and set the parking brake, letting the Ford Roadster idle.

""You cold, Hon?" he asked resting his arm across the back of her seat.

"Just bit," she shivered slightly.

"Here, let me crank up the heat…"

"Aren't we going in?"

"Not just yet…There is…something…." he paused for a bit, sitting quietly with one arm draped over the steering wheel and the other resting on the seat back behind her.

"I had a really good time tonight, Suzie." He smiled. She smiled back. Long ago she had decided it was useless trying to convince him she really hated that name. Coming from him, though, it didn't sound so bad.

"Yes. The Colonial Theater always outdoes itself in choosing the latest movies. *The Bells of St. Mary's* was excellent. I've always liked Bing Crosby. So, um, debonair."

"Ah, he's okay. Somewhat of a fop, I think. But as a priest, he was okay." He paused. "Listen, Suzie..."

"Yes, John?" She looked up at him expectantly. When he dropped his arm and hand resting behind her lightly across her shoulders, she nestled against him.

"I was wondering..."

"Yes? John?"

"Well, we've been going out now for, what? How many months now?"

"Since the middle of March. Nearly six months..."

"We like the same things, don't we?"

"Yes, mostly..."

"And we both like children? Don't we?" When she nodded, he stated, "Then I think we should think about having a baby!"

"John!"

"You do want to have one...or two, don't you?" he tried to tease. But there was a starkly intense seriousness in his voice.

"Perhaps. One...or two. In the future...But..." She knew what John was asking. What he had been pestering her about for the last three months.

"Well, now that the war is over and things are sorta getting back to normal...The world being a safer place and all that...Maybe we should definitely think about having one...or two." He paused, and then smiled. "I mean...after we are married, of course."

She nestled in closer, resting a hand softly against his rippled chest. "Is this yet another proposal?"

"I'd get down on my knee, but it's cold out. And you know how the left one bothers me..." he grimaced and then smiled wanly. Besides suffering a major wound in his shoulder when his B17 was shot down, he had twisted the joint slightly out of whack jumping out of the ball turret. The doctors at VFGH said it was nothing to worry about. But on cool crisp evenings like this one, it did sometimes bother him.

"No problem, John," Suzanne whispered. "You can bow before me later," she chuckled.

"Does that mean...yes?"

"I'll have to think about it..."

"You say that every time I ask you..."

"Yes. And every time I tell you that I am only

eighteen."

"You had a birthday this summer..."

"Okay. Nineteen. But, even so, I've hardly even dated any other boys...um, men. And, well, you are much older than I am."

"Five years is not that much..."

"It is to me...You've much more experienced than I..."

"You're mature for your age, Suzie. And I'm young at heart." He smiled and kissed her cheek. "And I always will be..."

"And you're consistently stubbornly persistent," she laughed, and then knitted her brow, finally making her decision. "And, you've worn me down..."

"I have? And does your using the past tense mean, dare I hope?" he grinned. "Yes?"

"Yes, John Joseph Voight the Second. I will marry you."

He let out a soft whoop. "Alright, then!" And then properly kissed his petite, pretty new bride-to-be. "Tomorrow," he promised, "we'll go to Yeager's Jewelers on Main Street and pick out your ring."

Suzanne's mother insisted on serving a nearly

formal dinner for both the Kessler and Voight families the next Sunday afternoon after church in celebration of her daughter's engagement. She hesitated when her eldest daughter told her she was asking Peggy Holmes to come. When her mother began to balk, that the dinner was "just for the immediate families", Suzanne flatly stated that right after their trip to Yeager's, she and John had stopped by the small Washington Street house to show off the solitaire one-carat diamond ring.

"I asked her to be my maid-of-honor. And she said yes. How much more family can that be?" For all intents and purposes, she considered Peggy, even if they weren't blood related, her sister.

"Well, you could have asked Ruth Ann!" Katrina Kessler bristled.

"She can be a bridesmaid."

"Who's getting married?" Ruth Ann asked, bounding down the stairs, her long blond braids flouncing over her shoulders. She wore one of her father's plaid flannel shirts with the tails hanging out over baggy blue jeans; the legs rolled up over scuffed, unpolished saddle shoes. Suzanne hated her sister's lack of fashion sense and informal style of dress.

"You look like an urchin tomboy," she quipped.

"Well, maybe that's because I am," the younger sibling quipped back, snatching a freshly baked oatmeal cookie from the pan Katrina had set on top of the stove to cool.

"That will spoil your supper, young lady," her mother scolded.

"Nyah! I'm a tomboy, remember?" Ruth Ann sassed between bites. "Thus, I have a growing tomboy's appetite." She snatched another cookie, and then frowned at Suzanne. "So, whose bridesmaid did you volunteer me for?"

"For whom did you volunteer me to be a bridesmaid," Suzanne corrected.

'Whatever," her sister said, munching around the rim of her second cookie. "These are exceptionally good, Mama. Are they for dessert?"

"They *were* for the coffee social after services tomorrow," Katrina said, exasperated by her daughter's unruliness.

"Mine," Suzanne sighed.

"What? You marrying that Johnny fella?"

"His. Name. Is. John." Suzanne said emphatically.

"And…yes, I am. Hopefully, next year. In early June."

"No way! I ain't getting gussied up in no frilly lady's dress for you. Ain't no way. No how. So there." She blew a raspberry at her sister. "Yuck to you!" she shouted as she scampered out the back door to the screened in porch. "Why do you hafta go breaking up our family like that anyway?!?"

"She is a handful, Mother," Suzanne said, politely asking if she might have a cookie, too. "If she won't be a bridesmaid, how did you even expect she would be a maid-of-honor?"

Katrina put two cookies on a small plate and set it in front of her now quite grown up child. *When did this happen?* she mused. *Nineteen years ago I gave birth, changed her diapers, and watched her learn to walk clinging to Abram's hand. Now, suddenly, she's an adult about to grace his arm to walk down the aisle…*

"Perhaps you are right," she sighed. "But I still object to Peggy standing up for you."

"Whom else would you suggest, Mama? And what do you have against her and Shanney Holmes?"

Katrina clattered around the kitchen for a few minutes, digging out pots and pans from overstuffed cupboards.

"Now that, my dear," she said, taking chicken quarters out of the refrigerator to bread and fry up for supper, "is a long story".

TWENTY-SIX

Ireland

While Shanney Holmes made a decent living as a blacksmith in County Cork, the shortage of food made staying in Ireland nearly impossible. After the Great War, which had taken its toll on the male population, blight had once again ravaged the potato crops and an epidemic of hoof and mouth disease had decimated the flocks of sheep and pigs. Fresh food was rarely available in the Saturday farmers market and, what little there was offered for sale, was expensive.

Shanney had been home for nearly two years serving in the Irish Brigades, but he still remembered the gnawing hunger and parching thirst suffered in the middle of a blood-soaked French battlefield. He was sick and tired of having to go through it all again. Like many of his fellow countrymen before him had decided, it was time to immigrate to America.

immigrate

A stubborn man, he could and would not be talked out of his decision. Not even by Martha, his wife of only six months.

Blight
Famine

"We just gotten settled in our new home," she argued. "I just finished making new curtains...And what about our families...my parents? I just...We can't just up and leave."

"Yes, we can," Shanney countered, taking off his leather apron and hanging it on a wooden peg next to the kitchen door. "And we will. If we're to start a family...I don't want my sons starving to death before they're even born..."

"The blight is bound to go away," she pleaded tentatively. "The crops will be better next year...The famine will end...You'll see...Have faith, Shanney. We can last until then..."

"Damn it, Martha! I won't wait another year! America is booming now! Don't you realize it's the promised land of milk and honey! We're going! Next month if I can snag the tickets."

He slammed his callused fist on the table, rattling the prized Dresden tea set her parents had given her as a wedding present. She caught one of the fine, hand painted cups before it crashed onto the rough-hewn wooded floor.

"Mind your temper, Shanney! Our china..."

"*Your* china be damned!" he yelled and with one

flowing sweep of his muscular sinewy arm, sent the tea set flying across the room. It smashed against the stone hearth, breaking into a million pieces. "We're going, woman! And that's final."

He watched as Martha stooped to pick up the fragments. She looked up at him with angry tears in her eyes. *At least,* she thought, *this time he struck the china and not me.* She rubbed the dark yellow bruise on her left cheek where he hit her in one of his angry, drunken rages a week ago. It was just beginning to fade.

"Yes, Shanney," she managed to say. "Anything you say. Sure, we'll go..."

"Good." He kicked a few shards with the toe of a hob-nailed boot, scattering them aside, and then clumsily, but lovingly reached down to help his wife up. "At least now," he said, "you have one less thing to pack."

Except for his leather apron and a small satchel of tools, Shanney sold the rest of his blacksmith equipment, including the anvil, iron forge, wagon, and his own two horses to pay for his and Martha's second-class passage on the *HMS Mary Elizabeth*. On Monday, March 20, 1922, they took the train from

Cork to Dublin

Cork to Dublin from whence the small steamer was ___ to sail the following day to Philadelphia.

Martha wanted to know why they weren't going to New York City where three of her cousins and their large families had immigrated five years ago. She had written to tell them that she and Shanney were coming to America. Would they meet them at the dock when the ship had landed? She also asked where there would be a good, decent place to live. But when she told Shanney about the letter she had just posted before their ship had sailed, her husband once again got angry and raised both his fist and his voice.

"I ought to crack you one for going behind my back..." he threatened. "I already made plans to settle in Pennsylvania." Martha cowered against a bulkhead, anticipating the blow. When two other passengers sauntered by, Shanney dropped his fist and lowered his voice.

He forced himself to remember that once, before he had enlisted, before he saw the ravages of war, before he experienced the horror of seeing many of his buddies fighting beside him senselessly, mercilessly killed, she was his pretty young childhood sweetheart.

Deep within his heart callused with anger, he knew he truly loved this sweet, bright, innocent, woman, now his adoring wife. He had to admit to himself, if not out loud to her, that he loved her more than life itself.

Oh, God help me, he prayed – to whom? To himself? – *Don't be such a mad fool, Shamus Patrick Holmes. Restrain yourself. What would I do if I lost her? God ever help me if I tried to hit her again.* He inhaled deeply and exhaled a long breath.

"Where we're going...It's horse country," he explained. "Much cleaner than those filthy, crowded New York tenements where those black Irishmen of your cousins live." Martha looked at him questionably. "I know. And had you asked me first, before writing that letter, I would have told you. I checked it all out. I want my sons to be raised in the country, not in some dingy, rat-infested city."

Martha nodded. Like she had promised in her marriage vows and the priest had quoted during this Sunday sermon the day before they left, "Whither thou goest, I will go..." She knew in her heart that while he vented his anger on her, he would be a good provider for their children.

"I had no idea...Shanney had a temper," Suzanne said, shocked at the story her mother was telling her. "He is always so calm, with a wonderful sense of humor. Like Dad...almost jocular."

"People can, and do change," Katrina explained to her daughter. "As often as chameleons change their colors. When I first met him, he was a violent man and poor Martha took the brunt of it. Then, when she...when she died giving birth to Margaret Ann...Well, it was too late for his sad remorse..."

"Why was he so angry?" Suzanne asked.

"Only the good Lords knows."

"I mean, he did love his wife, right?" She fearfully wondered if John would ever raise a hand to her once they were married. She had a few glimpses of his temper which he had so far kept in check. But John was a kind, gentle man at heart. She knew he would never hit her in anger; but will always caress her with love.

"Oh, yes. Very much so. And Martha...she loved her Shanney. Although, I had often wondered why..."

When Shanney was hired as an assistant blacksmith at the Phoenixville Iron Works, Martha found a four-room apartment on the third floor over Seacrist's stationary store on the corner of Gay and Bridge Street, close to the foundry and the shops downtown. Shanney had only to walk across the street to get to work in the morning and Martha had only two blocks to go for groceries. Using a bit of her lively Irish wit, she had also managed, to his surprise, to commandeer a small corner of the Seacrists' large backyard for a small vegetable garden.

Here in a small town, USA, he smiled to himself, *'tis sure we'll not be starving.*

"Abram and I had just gotten married and lived in the apartment below," Katrina explained. "Your father also worked at PIW...as an assistant engineer. When the Holmes moved in, we did our best to welcome them to the country and the neighborhood. But Shanney was a loner and despite Martha's outgoing nature, forbade her to associate with what he called, 'the wrong kind'. The wrong kind, indeed. The Kesslers and Borgs had been in Phoenixville long before those shanties arrived..."

"Ma!"

"Sorry...but...I get so angry when I remember..."

"When...how did you and Peggy's mother become friends?"

"When our husbands were at work, I'd go down and knock on the Holmes' door and ask if there was anything Martha needed. You see, there were those times, especially late at night, when Shanney stumbled home raving drunk; when we'd hear him below screaming and yelling at his wife...and..." she paused, wiping her eyes at the memories, "then...beating her. You just couldn't help hearing the screams all over the building. I often wondered why no one called the police...or why the Seacrists just didn't evict them.

"Your father tried at first to intervene, but Shanney wouldn't listen. He kicked Abram out of the apartment many a time until your father finally gave up. But Mattie and I were becoming close, like sisters. And I just couldn't let her be treated like that...I'd go down the next day when the men were at work, to help Mattie nurse her wounds and clean up the mess Shanney made throwing things around...at her. She was lucky he never broke any of her bones. But the bruises were sometimes quite ugly."

"Why didn't she just leave him?" Suzanne asked.

"In those days, it just wasn't done. A woman...A wife's duty was to stay with her husband. No matter what."

"So, what happened to Peggy's mom?"

"Well, we had to keep our friendship secret from Shanney, so we spent our days together helping each other with household chores, shopping in town, sharing books and magazines – both of us were great readers – and occasionally taking the bus to the state park in Valley Forge to stroll along the grassy expanses. We spent the nights apart, of course, alone with our husbands.

"When Martha finally became pregnant with whom Shanney hoped would be the first of many sons, the first person she told, after her husband, was me. I had to laugh because, you see, I was pregnant, too.

"A few nights later, Shanney came home drunk. And quite angry, as usual. He had gone out drinking with the boys from work to celebrate having a son.

For no reason at all, he beat Mattie unmercifully...I thought for sure she'd lose the baby...Or that it'd be damaged. But no, little Margaret Ann was born just a month or so after I had you."

"Perfect, of course..."

"Of course, just like you were...are...but..."

Suzanne blushed, then asked, "But?"

"Poor Mattie...Martha Holmes died a day later. They said she had internal wounds, probably from all the beatings, that had barely healed over time. Her body just couldn't take the strain of childbirth..."

Suzanne sat silently, her hand resting gently on her mother's arm, waiting for Katrina to dry her tears and relate the rest of her story.

"Despite everyone telling him to give the baby up, Shanney insisted on keeping her. I felt sorry for her...and, for some reason, for him. So, since I was still nursing you, I swallowed my anger and my pride and offered to wet-nurse little Peggy. Shanney was reluctant at first, but he really had no choice. I was in the apartment downstairs all day taking care of one baby...Why not two?"

"Mom, that is incredible. No wonder Peggy and I are like sisters! But why did you all these years forbid me to be friends with her?"

"I guess…I guess all of the good and most of the bad memories were, are still so strong. Especially since the few times I do see Peggy. She is so much like her mother." Katrina paused to dab her eyes again. "Well, Mattie was my closest and dearest friend…And I still miss her…

"And I'll…we'll never forgive Shanney for what he did to her! As far as you father and I are concerned, he practically murdered her…"

"But Mr. Holmes dotes on Peggy, Mom. He isn't angry…And I've never seen him drink…or drunk…"

"He stopped when Mattie died…Then, when I weaned Peggy, he bought that small house on Washington. We moved here to this large house shortly afterward. And then Abram and I decided we didn't want any further contact with the Holmes."

Suzanne's mother paused, and then stood up from the kitchen table. She smoothed her apron, poured oil into her large cast-iron skillet, turned up the gas flame under it, and began to bread the chicken quarters.

"If nothing else," she tried to smile, dipping a thigh into a raw beaten egg, "despite his kindness toward everyone, you ought to know that you father is not a forgiving man."

That next Sunday afternoon both the Kessler and Voight families, along with the Reverend "Pastor Freddy" Fromüeller, his wife, and their three rambunctious toddlers, sat down to what Abram later termed "...a royal feast". His wife had truly outdone herself cooking and serving the large sirloin roast, steamed vegetables, garden salad, freshly baked rolls, and warm apply strudel with French vanilla ice cream for dessert.

Margaret Ann Holmes, as Suzanne's best friend and maid-of-honor, also joined in the festivities. She sat next to the bride-to-be and applauded the many toasts to the young couple who were to be married next year in June.

Suzanne's parents had warmly welcomed her into the Kessler home with open arms.

TWENTY-SEVEN

It had taken Franz a week or so to settle into his work in the engineering department. He found *Herr* Kessler to be knowledgeable and affable, with a dry, droll sense of humor.

"See those tall brick towers on either side of the complex?" Abram asked the young prisoner of war the second day he had been assigned to what he termed his "care". "Those are the chimneys for the large furnaces that keep the hospital and, yes, your barracks, warm. It's my job, now yours...to keep them straight."

Franz frowned for a moment, trying to understand what he later realized was the joke that *Herr* Kessler was fond of repeatedly telling. He finally got it, but only after he had translated it into German and then back to English – *Meinen Job zu behalten, gerade* – keep them straight. Tall towers...straight up in the air. *That's funny*, he thought, and then softly chuckled to show his new supervisor that he appreciated his wit, however understated and misunderstood it might be.

Abram, in turn, was gratified to see that Franz also had a quick, yet quietly subtle dry wit. Over the days and weeks that they closely worked together, he also appreciated the young German's willingness to work and to learn new things. Franz was as equally adept at fixing things as he was tending to the patients, often solving in minute detail tricky maintenance problems with which even Abram had a bit of difficulty.

"There's this one boiler," the chief engineer explained to Franz. "She's very temperamental. She dies out every so often. Which shouldn't be, considering the boilers are fairly new. Each morning, I have to sweet-talk her into starting up. But not without a lot of stroking and cajoling...and cussing."

"These are basically steam engines? Like locomotives or big ships or farm tractors? *Ja*?"

"Yes, that is correct. Do you know how they work?"

"We had an old tractor on the farm back in Eisenach. It had a steam engine. It, too, constantly conked out and I learned at a very early age how to fix it...her." Franz smiled, remembering how his mother had also cursed and swore at "Benita", as his mother called it, the old *Benz SmokStak* with a similar engine as the hospital boilers, only a fraction of the size, when it died in the middle of the afternoon while she was plowing. He had raced out to the field with an oil-stained repair manual.

Two hours later, after much reading and a few too many failed attempts at starting it, he had mastered the inner workings. The tractor never again gave his mother any more trouble. And for dinner that night Gwen Weberhardt served her clever son an extra portion of spiced roasted pork, sauerkraut, and cinnamon-laced baked apples.

Perhaps the problem Herr Kessler was having with his huge boiler had the same solution as his mother's small tractor. "May I have a look at it?" he asked.

"Be my guest. You have the rest of the afternoon, until you have to go back to the stockade tonight, to fix it."

A few minutes before the guards were to escort the PW work details back to their compound for the evening, Franz beckoned Abram to the fusty boiler. He flipped a switch and it instantly started up.

"How did you do that?" Abram marveled.

"Magic?" Franz shyly smiled, wiping his greasy hands with a tattered rag. When he saw Abram's frown, he quickly added, "Just a matter of a starter coil about to burn out and a clogged feeder tube."

"Now why didn't I think of that?"

"Easily missed. The clog was deep into the tube...and the coil, the capacitor..."

"Never mind, my son. What matters is that you fixed it. And that she will last through the night...every night. Well done!" Abram gratefully enthused. "Well done!"

The next morning, Abram gave Franz a six-tube oil paint packet of the basic colors, four canvases stretched over homemade pinewood frames, and a handful of brushes.

"I heard you sketch...do a bit of oil painting," he explained when Franz gasped in astonishment. "This is in thanks for fixing ol' Bertha the Boiler. You are a very clever young man and I am sure you will put these to good use..."

"*Ja*...Yes. Thank you, but..."

"I saw the portrait you did of FDR for the patients tacked up on one wall of the blind wards, and I understand one of them, a patient, gave you his old art supplies."

"Tommy. Yes…"

"Well, here are some more. From my own studio."

"You, too, are an artist, *Herr* Kessler?"

"Of sorts. But, please, my name is Abram."

"Yes, *ja. Herr* Abram…*Danke.*"

"*Sie sind die meisten ganz herzlich willkommen,*" Abram smiled.

Franz nodded, amazed that the kind man had taken the time to give him a "most hardy welcome" in his own native language.

As the weeks wore on, they worked shoulder to shoulder maintaining the boilers as well as other machinery around the hospital complex. They joked about their work "keeping the towers straight".

Soon, as a strong bond began to form between them, Franz talked of his former life in Eisenach, his mother's farm, his medical studies at Efburt University, and, of course, Greta Hornweitz.

"But I haven't heard from them in more than a year," Franz said one day as Abram tinkered with one of the huge washing machines in a basement laundry.

"You can contact the International Red Cross, you know. Captain Templeton should be able to help you..."

"Yes, yes...but I've already told the Reverend Fromüeller and he has already contacted some committee of his church..."

"The Lutheran Commission for Prisoners of War."

"Yes, that's it. But they were not able, yet, to locate *mutter* nor Greta. It is hopeless..."

"Pastor Freddy is a good man. He won't stop his search until he has found them. Or what happened to them."

""Try turning that small nut there," Franz said, handing the engineer a small spanner wrench. "You know him?"

"I am an elder at his church, Bethany Evangelical Lutheran. I've known that kind pastor for years. He's a good man. Say, that did the trick, Franz. Is there anything you don't know how to fix?"

"My sadness, Herr Abram. *Ich Heimweh*. I am quite broken with homesickness."

"I can understand that. How long have you been

away?"

"A year at university," he attempted to count. "Less than one in the *Medical Korps*...two or more as a prisoner here...stateside..."

"I've never been homesick, Franz," Abrams counseled, replacing the machine's back panel. "Well, maybe a bit when I was serving in the Navy during World War One. Even then I was kept too busy maintaining the engines. There was no time to think of home, let alone long to be there. But...there are times when I do get sad. .And when I do, I paint memories..."

"Memories?"

"Of my childhood. My, um, younger days. You know, scenes of what Phoenixville was like before The Great War. This one as well..."

"What kinds of scenes?"

"Well..." Abram pushed his khaki workman's cap up so that the brim rested on his crown. "For instance, this land was once the Foster Farm. Before the family donated it to the War Department. Over one hundred and eighty acres. As a boy, I'd ride my bike here to buy milk and eggs for my mother.

"Over there," he pointed to the far edge of the

complex where the old, almost run-down farmhouse still stood and where Colonel Beakers with his small family now lived, "a massive twin-trunked ash tree loomed over the barn sheltering it and the cows and chickens in the pens and paddock. Very pastoral. Very calming."

"So you did a painting of it?"

"Yep. Hangs in our dining room. And someday," he asserted, "I will show it to you."

"If I am allowed."

"When you are allowed, Franz. The war is over and soon you will be free." Abram thought for a few moments. "Aren't there any childhood memories that you could paint?"

"Actually, I have started a painting of Luther sitting in the Wartburg Castle courtyard. I thought I'd give it for Reverend Fromüeller. He's been so kind to me. And his sermons are wonderful."

"Now, I know he'd really appreciate it."

"I don't think so. It isn't that good. I am doing a preliminary sketch, but I can't seem to capture...do it, Luther, justice."

"Why don't you bring it with you tomorrow? We'll take a look at it together."

When Abram saw the drawing the next day, he instantly recognized and appreciated Franz's talent.

"Well, you certainly are fastidious," he told the young artist. "You capture the minutest details in small, fine pencil strokes. An ability I wish I had." He knew young Franz's brush strokes would be just as delicate as he wanted his own, after many years of fine-tuning his own art, to be.

"So, you think it is good?"

"Very good. But what are the feelings you wish to convey...of Luther?"

"He was despondent...dejected...rejected. And also like me, quite *Heimweh*."

"Then, perhaps, he should be slouched on the bench, not sitting at attention."

"Not reading the book, just holding it...?"

"Yes. Gazing off into the distance..."

"...in thought and remembrance...*Ja*! That would work. Thank you, *Herr* Kess...er, Abram. *Danke schön*!

It was in Abram's comments that Franz realized the answer to his prayers about the painting. Even if it didn't come from Reverend Fromüeller.

"You are welcome," Abram grinned. "I cannot

wait to see the painting when you have finished it."

To Abram, their relationship was growing into a deep, abiding friendship. He took an interest in not only Franz's work in the engineering department, but supported him in his artistic endeavors. When there was the occasional lull in work, Abram made it a point to suggest that Franz "take a break" to sketch and paint.

To Franz, Abram was becoming the father figure he never had. But the young German did not mention his feelings. Instead, he showed his affection and appreciation by continuing to seek his advice about painting and working diligently alongside the chief engineer.

He made it a point to enthusiastically laugh at Abram's often repeated, sometimes nebulous, and, more often than not, unfathomable jokes.

TWENTY-EIGHT

When Pastor Freddy came to the prisoner's compound on Saturday mornings to worship with the prisoners, he was often accompanied by his three young children. All of them, while delighted to be with their father, were afraid of the "nasty German prisoners". He made it a point each time to comfort them, to tell them not to worry. The guards would protect them.

Sometimes, Abram would also attend the services to assist with the dispensing of Communion and distributing and collecting the hymnals. Knowing how the children must have felt, he also made it a point to sit with them in the back of the small chapel during the services, holding little Betty on his lap and the hand of her sister sitting beside him, all the while whispering words of comfort to their brother, the eldest Fromüeller child.

Attendance had been scarce for the first two or three weeks, but, with Otto and his bludgeoning insistence to keep it alive gone, the strict culture of the neo-Nazi regime in the compound eased. More and more of the German prisoners, especially the enlisted men, came forward on Saturday mornings to hear the words of Jesus Christ, the Gospel scriptures, and to reclaim their Christian faith, freeing it from the perverted ideology of the now deceased Hitler.

After a few months, Reverend Fromüeller mentioned to Abram that while he was pleased with the attendance of the enlisted members of the *Wehrmacht*, he wondered why only a few of the forty or so officers did not attend.

"I am not sure," was the reply. "Maybe you should ask one of the prisoners. Perhaps...Franz...?"

"Ah, yes. Our young artist. Good idea."

"Most of the *offizziers* still cling to their Nazi beliefs," Franz offered when Pastor Freddy approached him after services. "But I think that I will ask *Mein Freund*, Manheim, to attend. He is an officer and a doctor. Very well respected in our compound. If he comes, others might, too. But...I am not so sure...He might not agree..."

"Why not?"

"Well, he's not really Luth..." Franz caught himself, remembering the promise he made to his

Jewish friend.

"He's not really…What? Lutheran?"

"No, *nein*…Well, not…per se…but he is very spiritual."

"Well, than, what is he? Not that it matters. We Lutherans are very ecumenical."

"*Ja*. But…*Es ist nicht mein Geheimnis zu erzählen.* It is not my secret to tell."

TWENTY-NINE

Lieutenant Quisling and Sergeant Cooper were two of the twenty Army MPs assigned to guard the prisoner of war stockade. Unlike Cooper, who had no feelings one way or the other toward any of the captives, Quisling had a deep, abiding hatred for all Germans in general, especially one in particular. He railed against the deferential treatment the PWs received in what he called "The Fritz Ritz". Subtly mean and vindictive, he specifically singled out the "namby-pamby" Franz, resenting the preferred attention Abram Kessler and the Lutheran minister gave to the young German. When on duty he avoided what he called *those two-faced American Kraut traitors* and vowed to take vengeance on their protégé.

He spent two months monitoring Franz's every move, shadowing him to the engineering department each morning and trailing him back to Barracks 3 after supper each night, waiting for the right opportunity to wreak his revenge. Late one afternoon, when he was sure Franz would be staying late to help Kessler clean ashes out of the boilers and refueling them with coal, he snuck into Barracks 3 and stole the half-finished painting of Martin Luther at Wartburg.

Quisling smiled proudly at himself as he crossed the compound and scurried past the double rows of barbed wire fencing. He did not see Franz Weberhardt walk through another gate and stop in the shadows, surprised to see an Army MP sneaking out of the barracks carrying his painting. In the dimming twilight, Franz could not be sure which guard it was – although he had his suspicions – and was too frightened to accost the thief. He decided to tell Abram in the morning. *He will know what to do,* he thought. *I hope by then it is not damaged...*

When he got back to his own quarters, Quisling took a long look at the painting. *This is really quite good,* he reluctantly admitted to himself. *Even if it is done by that dirty, spoiled rotten German...As much as I hate to say it, it would be a shame to destroy it. Maybe I'll just keep the damned thing for now until I decide what to do with it.*

He stuffed the painting into a soiled pillow case and slid it under his cot. Proudly satisfied that he got away with his crime, he smugly strutted to the mess hall to find Cooper.

"It certainly looked like Quisling...I mean, his shape...and that arrogant swagger..." Franz said when he angrily told Abram. "He's been riding me ever since we left Fort Custer. More so now that Otto is no longer around..."

"I agree he is a smarmy guy. It might be wise to report the theft to Captain Templeton," Abram advised. "But to accuse Quisling when you don't know for sure it was him...He will only deny it and come after you. We don't want that, do we?"

Franz frowned as he clenched and unclenched his fists, not sure what to do.

"I supposed you are right," he reluctantly said. "But...my painting...It was almost finished..."

"Start another one. It will be better because you have practiced...And you have already seen with your mind's eye – and in oils – what you want to put on canvas."

Although he was still angry, Franz decided not to report anything to the Camp Commander. That night he started another version of his portrait of Martin Luther, using both his sketches and the image of the first nearly finished one in his mind as guides. This time, the painting went quickly. Almost feverishly painting with his short, deft, quick strokes, the young German knew his work would be completed in just a few days.

A week later, Lieutenant Quisling, surveying the prisoner's compound from atop the guard tower, watched Franz saunter from Barracks 3 to the engineering workshop. He was carrying an oil painting under his arm. *So, he's still painting, huh? Well, I think I'll steal that one, too,* he mused. *Start my own German art collection. Hah!*

The next afternoon, Quisling once again snuck into Barracks 3 and stole not only the painting, but the leather satchel of art supplies that Tommy, the young blind Merchant Marine, had given Franz. And once again he smiled proudly as he started to hasten back to his quarters.

Franz was coming up the gravel pathway when he saw a guard once again sneaking out of his barracks with the oblong canvas under one arm and the satchel in the other.

This time he was sure Quisling was the thief.

"Hey! Those are mine!" Franz shouted. He

lunged at the Army MP, slamming into his stomach, forcing Quisling to drop the painting and the satchel, spilling art supplies onto the ground.

They grappled for a few minutes, seemingly evenly matched, until the lieutenant managed to land a hard right cross on Franz's jaw. The young prisoner dropped to his knees in pain unable to avert the second blow to his chest.

Sprawled now on dusty stones, trying to catch his breath, Franz did not see the thick leather hobnailed boot raised to stomp on his left thigh, but he did hear the sharp crack when the lower part of the femur broke just above his knee.

Quisling panted as he ripped up the painting and tossed the pieces onto Franz lying unconscious in the dirt.

"Take that, you filthy German," he hissed, kicking the prisoner's side for good measure, then turned and walked away.

Quisling had already showered, changed into a clean uniform, and was on his way to downtown Phoenixville in search of whiskey by the time Franz was found an hour or so later by Sergeant Cooper.

The medics did not take Franz to the prisoner's

ward of the hospital. At the insistence of both Captain Templeton and Colonel Beakers, he was taken to the general hospital's emergency room. Once X-rays were taken and the extent of Franz's injuries were determined, Beakers immediately called for Dr. Manheim Zoloff

"He's the most competent bone surgeon we've got," he explained to his attending staff as he monitored Franz's vital signs. "Get him off that demeaning construction detail he is assigned to and get him back on our staff!" he barked. "STAT!"

"Even if he is one of *our* German *prisoners*?" the young American intern by his side snarked.

"The war is over!" the colonel snapped. "Give it a rest. This young man is no longer our enemy, but our patient. And, as such, he deserves nothing less than our best."

THIRTY

"The surgery went well, my young friend," Manheim said when Franz woke from the anesthetic and was resting reasonably comfortably in the orthopedic ward, his left leg in a long, hard plaster cast slightly suspended in a white canvas sling from the ceiling. "It was a compound fracture; easy enough for me to repair, but you will probably have a limp for the rest of your life. For now, bed rest for a few weeks, then a wheelchair..."

Franz winced at a twinge of pain.

"Yes, it will hurt for a while. I'll prescribe a pain killer..." Manheim paused. "Can you tell me what happened?"

"I will tell you, but no on else. Manheim, please. *De Bitte*. Please promise you'll keep quiet," Franz pleaded slowly, still groggy from the operation. "I am afraid if anyone else...knows."

"Ah, *ja*, my young friend. *Es ist nicht mein Geheimnis zu erzählen.*"

But now that he knew that it was Lieutenant Quisling who had beaten Franz up, Manheim decided otherwise. That evening after rounds he approached Colonel Beakers.

"Another damned prisoner incident," the Post Commander muttered. "You all seem to be more trouble then you are worth."

Manheim was taken aback by Beakers' assertion.

"You don't really believe that. Do you, Colonel? Sir?"

"No, sorry. I shouldn't have said that. But I don't believe one of Templeton's guards, whom I was assured are trustworthy and overly kind to our prisoners, would harm any of them."

"And I believe what Franz has told me! Why don't you?!"

The colonel bristled. *How dare a prisoner, even if he is one of the most talented surgeons I've seen, speak to me like that?* But he did not reprimand Zoloff. He had no objectionable response to the truth.

"I, too, am trustworthy," Manheim continued. "I have no reason to lie," he proffered, somewhat annoyed. *How dare this so called commandeer question my honesty? Just because I am his captive?*

"I don't doubt it, but...I agree that Quisling is a

bit of rake. But I have no reason to think he is guilty." Beakers paused. When the surgeon shook his head, he reconsidered. "If it makes you feel any better, I will have Captain Templeton conduct another one of his, um…'investigations'…But I doubt it will do any good. Knowing Quisling, he will only deny it. Will that satisfy you? *Herr Doktor Zoloff*?"

Despite Manheim being once again a trusted member of his staff, the colonel had an uneasy feeling that there was something the German officer was hiding.

"Yes, that is all I can ask. *Danke schön*."

"*De bitte*."

Just as Colonel Beakers had suspected, Captain Templeton's investigation into who attacked the young prisoner led to a dead end. When questioned, as expected, Quisling denied the accusation.

The following evening Lieutenant Quisling and Sergeant Cooper secured a few hours leave, "borrowed" an Army Jeep from the post motor pool, and drove into town to have a few drinks at Jennings Bar and Grill on Main Street.

Quisling eschewed supper and quickly downed two double scotches on the rocks while Cooper munched on a cheeseburger and fries and slowly sipped a cold Pabst Blue Ribbon.

Quisling began to talk freely about how much he hated the Germans and abhorred guarding them. The more he drank, the more he talked, and the louder he became.

"Sssh...lower your voice, Eric," Cooper said, finishing the last of his fries. "You're getting stares. Besides, you know how the captain is about security and secrecy..."

"Yeah, Augie, ol' pal," Quisling said, his speech beginning to slur. "Loose lips sink da ships...Well, let me tell you. I don't fucking care. I shoulda been sent oversees to kill a few of those damn Krauts instead of staying here and keeping them alive."

"Yes, well, that's the Army for you..." He took a small sip of his now lukewarm beer. "Come on, Eric...Maybe you should have something to eat to soak up all that liquor...Sober you up a bit."

"Don wanna get sobra..."

"Then I think it's time we drink up and go home."

"Nyah, I ain't finish yet. Gonna hab anudder. Then I'll tell you about the...the panshing..."

"The what?"

"That damn paneshing..."

"Painting? What painting?"

"Yep, two of them." the lieutenant said Then, in a slurred, garbled voice, he told the sergeant about the unframed, half-finished oil painting still hidden under his Army cot.

"Did you beat that young prisoner up?" Cooper asked. He knew Quisling had a bad temper. He had witnessed his vehement, hateful behavior toward the German prisoners when they were travelling from Fort Custer to Phoenixville and now guarding them in the Valley Forge General Hospital complex. Augie Cooper had long before suspected and was now certain that his drinking buddy was capable of doing just about anything.

"God damn it!" Quisling swore before he passed out cold. "What the hell do you think?"

Cooper prided himself on being, at heart, an honorable man. While Quisling was okay to occasionally have a few drinks with, he really had no use for the lieutenant's surly, superior attitude toward the PWs as well as their fellow guards. At first he thought he might leave Eric lying across the table for the MPs to pick up later, but decided that might not be such a good idea. Cooper hoisted the lieutenant across his shoulders in a fireman's carry, managed to cart the drunken officer to the jeep, and drove back to the hospital complex. *First thing in the morning*, he told himself, *I will report this to Captain Templeton.*

Quisling was in the shower when the sergeant and captain discovered the painting under his bed. When he walked in with just a towel wrapped around his hips, Cooper was standing beside Templeton, holding the painting.

"Well, I see you found it..." Quisling arrogantly said, taking off the towel and casually tossing it on the foot of his bed.

"Yeah, what of it?" Quisling sneered, then grinned, very slowly pulling on a pair of grey boxer shorts and a sleeveless undershirt. "It's just a stupid painting by a treacherous Kraut. Doesn't mean anything. No big deal, right?"

"Did you beat him up?"

"What?! Now why would I do that?"

"We know that you did," the captain said.

"No one saw me. You got no proof." He flicked his eyes between the captain and Sergeant Cooper. "Who told? You, Coop? Last night...that was crazy booze talk. You know me better than that..."

"Unfortunately," Cooper whispered. "I do."

"The prisoner," Templeton stated, "told his attending physician..."

"Who is also a dirty, stinking, lying German!"

"...and Doctor Zoloff told Colonel Beakers. Even though he is a prisoner, he is highly respected around here. A man beyond reproach..."

"So you say!" Quisling spat, zipping up his trousers.

"I think we have enough proof to have you court-martialed, Lieutenant. Hand over your pistol and rifle. Sergeant Cooper, take this man to the brig. We'll let him rot there until we can transport him to Leavenworth."

THIRTY-ONE

Abram was saddened by the loss of Franz's help in engineering. He missed the young man's eagerness to learn and to show off the progress of his painting. Most evenings after work before going home to his family, the engineer visited his young protégé, still bed-ridden, the upper part of his left leg and knee now encased in a thick plaster cast.

"Is there anything I can get you, Franz?" he asked.

"My painting was destroyed. I need another canvas...And my art supplies," Franz smiled, trying to sit up. "I have to start over. Once again."

"Third time is a charm," Abram quipped.

With Doctor Zoloff's assistance, Abram brought Franz's painting supplies and set up an small, make-shift easel from the arts and crafts building next to his bed.

"You are healing reasonably well, considering," Manheim said. "I think you can tolerate a few short hours in the afternoon sitting in a wheelchair to paint. Just as long as you keep that leg elevated."

Pastor Freddy visited late one Saturday morning after conducting services in the prisoner's chapel. He found Franz in his wheelchair carefully mixing various shades of red for Luther's long, velvet robe.

"I missed you at services today," he offered. "But I understand why you didn't, couldn't come. I heard what happened and thought I'd stop by." He leaned over to look at Franz's work. "Say, that is really good. Better than the first...?"

"And second," Franz smiled. Despite the uncomfortable cast, the sharp stabs of pain, and the prospect of a long recovery, now that he was able to paint he felt his life was coming back together again. And, he was beginning to rediscover his own sense of humor.

"Do you really like it?"

"Yes, of course. I really like it," the reverend said, taking a small, yet thick blue-dyed leather-bound book out of his pocket. "Since you are doing a portrait of Luther, I thought you'd like to read about him, his life, and why and how he started the Reformation." Reverend Fromüeller hesitated. "Well, that's not quite true. He didn't start it, per se, so much as he was very instrumental in fostering it…"

Franz turned to the cover page. *The Life and Times of Martin Luther* by J. H. Merle D'Aubigne.

"He was a French clergyman. Wrote this in 1846. A gentleman named H. White translated it into English. It's a bit of a hard read…but…"

"What little I know of Martin Luther I first learned in Sunday School," Franz explained. "What I told you before, his feelings as a prisoner…Everyone in Eisenach knew the story of him being held in the fortress. That part is common knowledge and I frequently explored the castle and spent long hours in the courtyard. I surmised how he must have felt…"

"And the rest of his life?"

"When Hitler ordered the churches closed, my mother tried to continue to teach me. We are Lutheran, yes, but she relied more on her faith than on her limited knowledge…"

"Exactly what Luther believed and taught. And it's all there…in the book."

"Then I shall enjoy reading it, Pastor Freddy. Thank you for lending it."

"No, no. Keep it. I insist. It is yours," he smiled "Now, how about we offer a few prayers for your quick recovery?"

As Franz bowed his head, clutching the thick little tome in his hands, he knew his intention of eventual thanks toward the Lutheran minister was on the right track.

Over time, Franz's broken femur healed, but not well-enough for him to be able to return to the strenuous duties working with Abram. Manheim reiterated that he would always walk with a limp; often with the aid of a cane. For the rest of his life, he would have a not-so-gentle reminder of Quisling's hatred and cruelty.

Instead of a regular work detail, Franz was asked to help with the arts and crafts classes, assisting recuperating American patients as well as those German prisoners who were interested to learn to draw and paint. And while he would miss working with Abram, he could now spend almost all of his time on his latest creation.

With Lieutenant Quisling court-martialed and now in prison, he rejoiced. Finally, there was no longer any threat of harassment.

THIRTY-TWO

Sergeant Major Daniel George Harrup had been extraordinarily proud of his new rank and his subsequent assignment as one of two resident ophthalmologists at Valley Forge General Hospital.

Two days after graduating from Harvard Medical School in 1942, he had enlisted in the Army Medical Corps. He spent thirteen weeks in grueling infantry and specialized training at Camp Edwards in western Massachusetts and, in mid-September, three days after receiving his commission, he decided to cut short his ten-day leave and report for duty at the Army recruitment and assignment center in Boston's old Farmer's Market terminal building.

The lines had been long that unusually chilly September morning, wrapping around the building and down Market Street. Daniel stood shivering in the middle of one of the shorter ones, dismayed that he would have to wait for hours, longer than he had anticipated, before he was called into the building. Not a patient man, Daniel shifted his feet and stretched his long, stocky back from side to side, not so much to keep warm, but to stem the boredom.

The assignment line he was in crept slowly toward the large double doors until he and four other Army Medical Corps officers were finally ushered into the old terminal and ordered to stand together in a row in front of a long, wooden trestle table draped in red, white, and blue bunting. A craggy, graying, somewhat elderly officer, his Army uniform festooned with ribbons and medals, sat behind the makeshift desk. His thick jowly jaw gently bobbed on his chest. *Geez,* thought the newly commissioned doctor, *he looks asleep.*

"Good God, he must be older than Methuselah," a staff sergeant next to Daniel whispered. "No wonder we had to wait so long..."

"We were kept waiting out in the cold for hours until that old coot wakes up from his morning nap?" Daniel groused. He looked around, frowned at the crowd of eager recruits inside and decided he wasn't going to wait any longer. *Perhaps if I come back tomorrow morning,* he thought to himself, *the lines wouldn't be as long...nor as slow. And maybe there'll be a much younger officer sitting behind the desk.* He nodded to his companions, smiled wanly at the elderly officer who finally harrumphed and grumbled as he began to shuffle application forms and various protocol assignment manuals on the makeshift desk. *Besides, technically, until I do report, I am still on leave.*

"Don't think I can wait any longer," Daniel said. "See you all in the funny papers..."

As he turned to go, a young, pretty, red-headed woman in a clean crisp, though slightly faded Women's Army Corps uniform stood behind him and reached up to tap his shoulder. At six feet six inches, Daniel towered over just about everybody. He turned and looked down. The WAC Corporal held a clipboard in one hand and what looked like a telegram in the other.

"Excuse me, sir, Sergeant Major...Sir!" she said in a dry, thick Boston accent looking up at him. From Amish country himself, Daniel could barely understand what she was saying, despite his six years spent living and studying in Cambridge. "Don't leave yet..."

"Why not? I've waited long enough for...um, this man's army," he quipped. Might as well make light of the situation. "Maybe tomorrow..."

"Ah, but that would be too late, I am afraid. It must be today."

"What? Why today?"

"I am the assignment's officer's assistant," she smiled, tilting her head ever so slightly toward the elderly gentleman. "General Bassett is retired, you know...but tries to help out here as best he can when we're understaffed. He's, um, not quite himself today...."

"I can see that," Daniel said impatiently. "Couldn't they have gotten a younger, somewhat more awake officer to do the processing?"

"Most of them are on the front lines..." she frowned. "Besides, if you would just wait a minute...I can help you."

He looked askance at her, noticing that her dark green eyes, despite her furrowed brow, were smiling, no, twinkling at him. "Shoot..." he shyly smiled back.

"This wire," she said, holding up the telegram. "A new post just opened up for a residency at the Valley Forge General Hospital in Phoenixville."

"Where?" Daniel frowned quizzically. Then he smiled. If what he heard was true and if what he thought was going to happen...He just couldn't believe his luck.

"Phoenixville. That's in Pennsylvania..."

"Yes! I know exactly were that is. My paternal grandmother, Samantha Harrup, lived, er, lives there..."

"Well, then...in that case. Would you like to accept?"

"Yes!" he nearly shouted, bouncing on the balls of his feet. "Yes! Sir! I most certainly would!" he exclaimed. "When do I report? Sir?" he asked, and then smartly saluted.

"No need for that, *Sir*," the WAC smiled at the new officer insignia carefully sewn onto his sleeve, and saluted back. "Give me half an hour and I'll have you signed up and your transfer papers ready. You leave on the 5:43 hospital train tomorrow morning..."

That was nearly three years ago, Dr. Harrup mused, gazing out of the large window of the laboratory. The sky had turned a milky grey. Small snow flakes started to lazily drift past the window down to the wide expanse of grass that fronted the research center. *It was snowing when I came here, too*, he smiled wistfully. *A lot has certainly happened since th*en.

For one, he had successfully completed his one-year residency, was appointed assistant to the department head and, now, when he was not taking care of patients visually impaired and blind due to wounds sustained in the war, he worked on what Dr. Zeb Rowan called "a most interesting and much needed invention...The men who have lost eyes – and their confidence – will be thrilled!" With Zeb's occasional help, Harrup had completed most of the work during the last six months. Just a few more finishing touches were all that was needed.

Valley Forge General Hospital, of all places! he thought, watching the snow accumulate. *I still can't believe my luck, being in the right place at the right time when that pretty WAC officer spotted him. Well, I do stand out in a crowd.* He chuckled to himself, remembering the look on her face as she had to stand on tip-toe to talk to him.

With his sturdy, 6'6" muscular frame, the young man towered over everyone. *How could she not have spotted me? I wonder what ever happened to her?* He made a mental note to look her up the next time he was in Boston. *Sure,* he smiled. *But first I'll have to remember her name.*

Doctor Danny, as his mother and younger sister teasingly dubbed him when he was last home to Hazelville on leave, sighed and turned away from the window. This past February he had watched through the same window as seven lorries carrying members of the German *Medical Korps* slowly drove by on their way to the stockade. It was, he recalled, snowing then, too.

He settled on a tall lab stool to continue his work. He had just an hour or so before he had to return to the wards to do rounds with Dr. Rowan and Colonel Beakers and then, after that, a meeting with a young prisoner in the arts and crafts building. *What was his name again?* Dr. Harrup tried hard to remember. *Hans? Kurt?. Witzshel? No. Let me think. Franz. Yes, that's it! Franz. Franz Weberhardt. Yes...yes...He said he had an idea for my invention...I wonder what it could be.*

He delicately lifted one of the small, stark white, unmarked balls of acrylic from the small cooling rack on the lab table and held it gently between his thick thumb and forefinger.

"Yes…Yes," Doctor Danny muttered to himself, gazing at it. "I am hoping that this little fellow will change patients' lives. Not bad, for the youngest son of a poor coal miner still digging for anthracite in the central Appalachian Mountains of northeastern Pennsylvania. Not bad at all."

An hour later, during which Danny had formulated a basic plan for customizing the size of the artificial eye for each patient using a mold fashioned out of cotton dipped in wet plaster and then wrapped in gauze, he scurried down one of the corridors toward Ward 45; his long, white coat flapping behind him. As he hurried, he tried to remember at each hall junction which way to turn. Even after three years of daily using the corridors and tunnels that connected all of the hospital buildings together, he still easily got lost in the maze.

"What do you know about a young prisoner?" Daniel asked Colonel Beakers as they walked between patients. "Name is, um…Franz Weberhardt, I think."

"Ah, Franz! The young painter. Very talented,"

the colonel said quietly, watching Dr. Rowan lift the eyelid of a Navy midshipman and shine a small light through the iris.

"Can you see that, son? No? A bit? Just a bit. More shadow then dark? *Ja*? *Ja. Das ist gut.* Very good. A week or so, I think," Dr. Zeb – as he was affectionately called by the staff and his patients – smiled. He motioned for a nurse to replace the white gauze bandages. "Make sure he gets the drops twice a day," he ordered.

"Franz..." Colonel Beakers continued as they ambled toward another bed. "Is well-liked by every one here...helps with the arts and crafts now that most of our other prisoners are no longer allowed...er, involved with the care of the patients. I am surprised you haven't bumped into him before. Why do you ask?"

"A painter. Huh," Daniel said, more to himself than to the Chief Medical Officer. Mostly voluntarily sequestered in his lab, he had made it a point in the last eight or nine months to avoid contact with the prisoners, keeping any involvement with them to a minimum. His decision to remain aloof was more so to honor his grandmother's wishes than being faithful to his own convictions.

Samantha Harrup was not the sort of woman who was able to keep her feelings, emotions, highly opinionated moralistic ideals, nor her dry, though often caustic, sense of humor to herself. She had passed on the latter to her only grandson and used the former traits to bitterly complain about the failures of her only son who succumbed to the allure of alcohol and cigarettes and eventually found himself spending long, arduous days under the mountains resurrecting fossils for fuel.

It was her money, inherited from her late, dearly departed husband that, with the help of a few conniving attorneys, she had kept it from her son and set up the scholarships that had paid for Daniel's sojourn at Harvard.

And here he was now, on one of his first afternoons off from work, standing in her mid-Victorian style entrance foyer, a tall, strapping young man – an Army officer and a fine doctor at that! – grinning from ear to ear.

"Hello, Grandma!" Daniel exclaimed delighted to gather his father's aging thin and wiry, but not yet frail mother into his strong arms. She wriggled free and quickly led him to the camel-backed horsehair sofa in her front parlor, eschewing his usual request for a three-finger glass of single malt. He had to settle for a small crystal glass of nearly sour sherry.

"You, know, Danny," she snorted, "that my best friend is Evie G. Radnor, one of our borough's older leading socialites..."

"How could I ever forget her?" Daniel smiled. He knew she had lost her son, one of his high school classmates who decided to enlist rather than go to college, in the Battle of the Ardenne.

"Well...she wrote the letter to the editor of *The Daily Republican*...that resulted in the reassignment of the prisoners from hospital to menial work. In many respects, I agree with her ideas. But having not lost anyone to the war, I am not all that unkindly unsympathetic..."

"What is your point, Grandma?" he asked impatiently. He really did not have the time or the inclination to hear one of her many conservative lectures on the state of the war. Especially if he had to sip sherry instead of scotch.

"I am, in some ways, glad for the extra help of

the German prisoners – medical personnel – to assist the short-staffed hospital..."

"Yes? And?"

"However, I wish not for you to be involved with them..."

"That can't be avoided, Grandmamma," he protested. "We're all to work together for the good of the patients..."

"But still, will you promise?"

"I can only promise you that I will try. But that may not be so easy. Some of the German medics are quite capable...and quite well-received by the staff. I suspect I will be one of them..." When she glared at what she considered his impudence, he said somewhat condescendingly, politely pretending to sip his drink. "That's all that I can do, Grandma. Promise to try. No guarantees."

On the bus ride back to the hospital, he wondered what her true objections were to his "fraternizing" with the enemy prisoners. Surely, they can't all be as bad as she had intimated. Still, he would try to make it a point to avoid them.

That was then, he frowned to himself as he

continued participating in the rounds with his colleagues and the Chief Medical Officer, anticipating his meeting afterward with the young prisoner. *This is now. And regardless of her previous objections, Grandmamma will never know.*

Dr. Harrup nodded as they approached an Army officer fully dressed in his light khaki uniform sitting on the edge of his bed. A small suitcase sat on the floor beside his feet. A large gauze bandage was taped to the right side of his forehead, just over his eye.

Captain Honeywell was one of Daniel's luckier patients. He recalled that a bullet had grazed his temple while leading his men in the heat of battle over the crest of a hill outside of Arles, traumatizing a few nerves. The captain had lost his eyesight from the damage. But, now, after a few months in Danny's care, except for the nasty scar, he was completely recovered.

"Discharge day today," the captain said quietly.

"Yes, I know. I signed the papers this morning. Not going back to France, I understand?" Doctor Danny asked.

"Nope. I am finally going home. Remember, sir,

Hitler shot himself and his wife in their filthy bunker in April and the Nazis surrendered in May. The war is over..."

'Yes, right," Dr. Harrup smiled, flustered by his mistake. He should have remembered, but didn't. "Yet, we've so many wounded to take care of...and they still keep coming...I, we have been quite busy...I tend to forget."

"Not a problem, Sir. It's to be expected after all we've been through. It's been a hard four years. Very hard."

"Good luck, Captain," Daniel smiled, moving away from the bed. He then turned to Colonel Beakers.

"This Franz has asked me to meet him after rounds, sir," he explained, remembering to refrain from using the more familiar "Hank" the colonel preferred to be called when they were not on duty. "I am just a little concerned..." He noticed the puzzled look on Dr. Rowan's thin face. "I think he has an idea for my...er...our invention. But I can't fathom what that might be..."

"Don't worry, Danny. You'll enjoy meeting Franz," Colonel Beakers said. "He's not like most of the other prisoners…Very quiet, unassuming…But so very talented! Sad, though, after all he's been through here…"

"What, Sir?"

"I surmise you've not heard that, too, squirreled away as you are in your ivory-towered lab when you're not with patients…working on…perfecting a white ball of acrylic…" the colonel said, mildly sarcastically. He paused. He was not all that enthusiastic as his other two staff members were about the idea of an artificial eye made of semi-soft plastic. When Zeb and Danny first told him about the idea, he pooh-poohed it, turning, as it were, a jaundiced eye. "I'll believe it when I see it," he had gruffly said, unaware of the pun.

"Franz," he continued, "was badly beaten by one of our guards…Broke his right femur clean through, just above the knee." As they walked down one of the connecting corridors to Ward 50 he told Danny about Zoloff, the "cracker-jack" German orthopedic surgeon who had "pinned him back together rather nicely."

Beakers explained that Franz was out of the hospital now, but still in a wheelchair. "He won't be able to use crutches for at least another month...But he's pretty chipper about it. Spends his time when not teaching painting mostly around the stockade and chatting with Abram Kessler, our engineering guru down by the furnace stacks...always drawing, painting. And he has taken quite a fancy to arguing the finer points of theology with Reverend Fromüeller..."

"What do you mean, 'he's not like some of the other prisoners'?" Danny interrupted.

"Oh, you'll see," Beakers said kindly, reaching up to assuredly pat Danny on the shoulder. "Keep an open mind. Give him a chance. You'll see."

Danny walked briskly through the falling snow toward the back of the hospital buildings where the prisoner stockade had been built and where the two buildings that housed the recreation facilities for both patients and prisoners alike were. He hiked up the collar of his woolen Army great-coat and stuffed his large hands deep into his pockets as he lumbered along. His tall, slightly husky frame huddled against the brisk wind starting to career off the makeshift soccer field the prisoners had constructed the beginning of last summer.

He found the lithe, frail Franz Weberhardt sitting in his wheelchair in front of a large easel, lightly daubing small flecks of blue paint with a thin bristled brush on a small canvas. He did not wish to disturb the young artist at work just yet and stood just inside the door, watching silently as Franz speckled the scene with graying clouds laced with faint orange, pink, and dark yellow streaks of an approaching sunset and then dabbled froths of white on the water below. A small boat – was that a schooner? – seemingly bobbed on the waves.

"It's okay, Doctor Harrup," Franz said in his thick northern German accent as he worked. "*Bitte.* Please. You can come closer. I don't bite." He laughed and then, with a bit of difficulty and some pain, turned to look behind him. He held the brush poised over one shoulder as he glanced at his visitor. "Sorry I can't get up to properly greet you. But, as you can see…"

"That's quite alright, Franz," Danny said. "Hank…er, Colonel Beakers told me what happened to you…"

"Yes, well. It's all over now and Quisling is

serving time at Leavenworth. And I...well, I am serving time in this...this..." he slapped the wooden arm of the wheelchair, grasping it to stem the tide of the last remnants of his angry hatred. "I just can't work with Abrams anymore. Besides being with the patients, which I loved most of all. Being with him. Working on the boilers. Fixing things Hauling coal, the ashes...I enjoyed all of it. Very much."

Danny winched when Franz said, "hauling coal". He knew that his aging father was still working down in the Hazelville mines, despite his mounting, debilitating symptoms of emphysema. He pictured Horace Harrup's shoulders cowered as he hauled buckets of anthracite up the steep, narrow passages...trying to make enough money to feed his large family. Danny shuddered and shook his head to clear his mind of the image...

"Sorry, Doctor Harrup," Franz said, a look of concern crossing his face. "Are you alright? Is something wrong?"

"No, no. Please, I am fine," the young ophthalmologist slowly said. "Please, um, call me Danny. We're not working. It's off hours. What are you painting?" he asked, tentatively coming closer to peer at the canvas.

"Before I was captured, we were camped near the Volturna River. In Italy. I remember this scene," he indicated the painting with the brush, "The night before the battle...sitting in the early evening, waiting for the sun to set...a breeze came up...and the schooner sailed by. It seemed so peaceful and I thought then I would like to capture it in oils...See?" he said, showing Danny the sketch he had made from memory on a small pad while sitting at the river's edge. "I did draw it...but in pencil. No colors..."

"It's quite good," the young doctor smiled, admitting he really had no knowledge of what constituted good – or even bad – art. "A bit impressionistic, isn't it?"

"Yes, I am a fan of Monet and Degas...and van Gogh. But...I lean more toward realism. Like my portrait of Luther..."

"Luther?"

"Martin Luther. At Wartburg Castle. In 1521. Surely you know the story?"

"Um, no. Sorry. I am not that religious. Raised a Baptist, I think...But I never professed let alone practiced my faith. Too busy with other things, I guess."

"Not a problem, as you Americans say." Franz wheeled himself over to a table and invited Danny to sit across from him. A few bottles of cold Schlitz beer, saved from his weekly allotment, were on the table with two tall, iced pilsner glasses. "Sorry this isn't anything more, um, stronger, but...Would you like a drink?"

"Sure, Franz," Danny smiled, realizing that he had quite uncharacteristically taken an instant liking to this fine young man whom, had the war not ended a few short months ago, would have been considered "the enemy". *Colonel Beakers...Hank*, he reluctantly admitted, *was right. Franz Weberhardt is, indeed, different.* He watched as who he hoped would be a new friend pour from one of the bottles and hand the cool glass to him.

"So," he began. "You asked me here...Because?"

"Well, I wanted, first of all, to meet you, Danny. You are quite an elusive member of the American hospital staff despite your, um, *presence*," Franz smiled. "And then...to tell you of my idea. For your invention."

Danny slowly took a long, thoughtful draught of his Schlitz, savoring the slight acrid bitterness. He set the now half-full glass on a small cloth napkin on the table in front of him, gently turning it between his massive fingers.

"How did you...a prisoner...know about that?"

"After my operation and a month of healing, I was able to wheel around the hospital. Last month, I was rolling around the burn and blind wards where I used to nurse patients and I found one patient who became a friend, actually. Tom. He lost sight in one eye and the other was totally destroyed. It had to be removed."

"A young Merchant Marine?"

"Yes, you know him?"

"One of my patients." Danny leaned back, took another sip of beer, amazed at what he was now coming to believe were planned coincidences in life. *But by whom?* "With only one blind eye, too afraid to leave to go home...His self-confidence is completely shattered. With an empty socket, he feels he is too disfigured to, um, see, be with anyone. But then...I did tell him about my new acrylic eye..."

Franz sighed empathically and then said,

"Yes...he told me about your suggestion. All that you said. But he rejected the idea, didn't he? Well...I think we, together, can help him to accept it. Here's my idea."

Franz expounded on the pain caused by glass eyes that, used for the last two hundred or so years to mostly ease the discomfort of others seeing the disfigurement of those afflicted with the lost of an eye. Soft plastic would be so much less painful and more comfortable to wear.

"Patches, yes, are fine. Sort of...Well...but a plastic eye would also be so much more aesthetic, if nothing else...Only, if..." He paused, smiling at Danny as he finished his beer. He opened another bottle and refilled each of their glasses.

"If the artificial eye had an iris, a corona and...veins." He took turned the pages of the sketch pad to the middle. "Somewhat like this." The multi-colored sketch was a fine, detailed representation of a human eye.

"But," Danny said, shaking his head, not quite fully comprehending what Franz was trying to tell him.

"You...I mean, I would draw, paint with, um

acrylic colors on your acrylic eye exactly what it would look like. Perfectly matched to the patient's other eye. See? Veins, iris, and all. I'd be happy to do that for you. At least for the first models you make. "

"You mean, a prototype…"

"*Ja.* So, we make together the first one for Tommy?"

Danny studied the sketch more closely and carefully considered Franz's idea. Indeed, it did have more than just some merit. He finished off the second glass of Schlitz in one gulp and then said, "Brilliant! Yet, so simple. Why didn't I think of this?"

He thought for a moment, and then said, "Once I've perfected the mold, I could fit Tom in two weeks. Then you can paint the details on his new eye."

THIRTY-THREE

When not with John, Suzanne spent the better part of her weekends with her mother and her maid-of-honor planning the wedding, tentatively scheduled for the beginning of next summer. Leaving the details of the actual ceremony to the Reverend Fromüeller, who promised a great deal of pomp and circumstance – at least as much as the tenets of the Lutheran synod would allow – they planned a sumptuous luncheon reception afterward at the Columbia Hotel on upper Bridge Street.

With the war finally over and the strict rationing of meats lessened, they decided upon rib-roast, scalloped potatoes, steamed vegetables and, de rigueur, the traditional four-tiered wedding cake with lemon-vanilla icing for dessert. The flavor selected in deference to John's almost insatiable sweet-tooth. Caught up in the excitement of her first daughter's wedding plans, Katrina and Suzanne spent two full November Saturdays scouring countless Philadelphia bridal shops in search of "just the right dress".

Amidst all the frenzy, the two young women volunteered to help with the United Services Organization. Peggy had already joined its choir that summer and had convinced Suzanne to join her in "entertaining the troops". They sang in the USO Christmas concert for service men from the hospital: staff as well as those patients who were able to attend. The local USO hall, on the far corner of Bridge and Gay diagonally across from Seacrist's, was packed that Saturday evening before the New Year.

Those from the ophthalmology wards were guided by nurses and borough residents who had volunteered to help the blind and partially blind practice their newly found navigational skills in town. Standing in the alto section on a riser overlooking the audience, Suzanne recognized a few of them who escorted patients as they strolled through downtown Phoenixville, white canes tapping; shopped in local stores; ate hot pastrami sandwiches at Malone's Deli; and worshipped on Sunday mornings at Bethany Evangelical.

"That was fun," she said to Peggy afterward. "When's the next big event?"

In February, the local USO hosted a Valentine's Day dance for both patients and hospital staff. Suzanne's father, who had also attended with her mother, made it a point to stand at the door to greet the staff members, as well as some of the patients who had become regular Bethany parishioners.

She was so busy taking turns dancing with servicemen and John, she did not notice the few men in PW uniforms lingering near the refreshment table. This time the USO invitation was extended to those German prisoners who had exhibited good behavior and had proved trustworthy.

With the war over, Colonel Beakers had eased restrictions on the prisoners, often allowing them to accompany patients and nurses into town. He had restored some, like *Herr Doktor* Manheim Zoloff, to their original work details in the wards treating and caring for American servicemen.

Franz, too, had proved exemplary and was recommended by Abram and Pastor Freddy to attend the dance. Albeit on crutches, he had been allowed to guide Tommy, now smiling, proud of his new acrylic eye that Franz had painted to exactly match the other.Strains of a lively Cole Porter tune wafted through the hall from the live band on the small stage. Enjoying the chance to dance the fox trot with her husband-to-be, Suzanne glanced up into John's face as he expertly guided her across the dance floor. Intent on etching the moment into her memory, she did not see Franz smiling at her from across the room.

How could I forget, he thought, *those dusty blue-grey eyes? So like Greta's…That is the young woman I saw waiting for the bus so many months ago. I wonder if she would remember me?* When the music stopped, he made his way slowly, cautiously across the room to where Suzanne was now sitting at a table with John and a few members of the hospital staff. He silently stood behind her slightly to her left for a few minutes, unnoticed until he gently touched her shoulder with his fingertips.

"*Entschuldigen sie bitte.* Excuse me, please, *Fraulein.* You may not remember me, but, I saw you when…"

John jumped up from his seat and grabbed the prisoner's arm. "How dare you accost her!" he shouted, knocking Franz's hand away. He rose up on tip-toes to stare the German down. Even stooped over his crutches, Franz's lithe frame was at least a head taller. He smiled shyly and tried to explain.

"*Es tut mir leid, aber...*"

"Speak English, you...you..."

"John, please..." Suzanne whispered. She put a hand on John's back, trying to restrain him. "Don't make a scene..."

Everyone in the USO hall stopped what they were doing and watched the drama unfolding at the small table to the left of the stage. Abram started to approach John and Franz to avert what appeared to be the start of a fight, but was stopped by Katrina who grasped his hand.

"No, Abram. It's no longer our place to protect our daughter. That, now, is John's."

"I am not making a scene!" John snapped at Suzanne. "This, this *German prisoner* is!"

Franz chose to ignore John and turned to Suzanne. "I am sorry, *Fraulein*. But we have met."

"Where?!" John demanded. "Suzanne?!"

The face did look familiar. She tried hard to recall where she had first seen it.

"I was in the back of a lorry..." Franz tried to explain as John started to push him away.

"I don't care where you were...But I do know where you are now...and where you are going!" John exclaimed. "Get out of here before I throw you out!"

"*Fraulein, fraulein*, please...*sie bitte*..." Franz said, extending his hand to her. "I just want to talk with you..."

"I told you to leave her alone!" John shouted, and then punched Franz in the gut. The blow threw the prisoner off balance, toppling him over. His crutches clattered on the floor beside him. "Now, get up and get out!"

"John!" Suzanne shouted. "How could you? A defenseless man like that..."

"Defenseless? A German with American blood on his hands? Who probably murdered many of my buddies? I don't think so!" He scoffed, and then rubbed the knuckles of his right hand with his other palm. He squared off and faced Franz, fists poised and feigning punches at the ready. "Come on, Kraut! Want more? Then get up, or crawl out."

Two of the hospital staff and one of the other prisoners rushed to help Franz stand and escort him out of the building. Abram glared at Katrina and then at his daughter who still clung to John's arm as he shadow boxed. He hastened across the dance floor and clasped the younger man's shoulder.

"That's enough, son. I think you can stop now. And, I suggest you calm down and apologize to Suzanne."

"I don't need his apology, father," his daughter said, her head bowed, trying to fight back her tears. "I know he has a temper...But I do remember who the prisoner is," Suzanne tried to explain. "He was the one I saw that first day...in the back of the lorry..."

"I don't care, Suzanne, where you met...him. I don't like you fraternizing with the enemy!" John said, clenching his teeth.

"I was not fraternizing. And...he is not the enemy. The war is over, John. Remember?"

"Maybe for you..."

"Okay, you two," said Abram. "Maybe you should take some time apart, okay? Suzanne, you will come home with you mother and I. John, I suggest you go somewhere and cool off. Tomorrow you can come by the house to apologize."

"But..." John saw the look in Abram's eyes and the disappointment in Suzanne's. He sighed angrily, then turned on his heels and walked away.

The next morning in church, Suzanne sat with her parents and younger sister instead of sitting with John as she usually did since they became engaged. She avoided looking at him although he tried to catch her eye a number of times during the service. Afterward, her father whisked her away.

"When he is ready, he will come to his senses and apologize. Until then..."

"Yes, I know, Da. Best to stay apart." She then asked about the fair, sandy-haired young German. "Do you know him?"

"He is...was my assistant in the engineering department who I told you and Katrina about. Franz Weberhardt."

Suddenly all the pieces began to come together.

"I would like to meet him, father," she said. "And apologize for John's behavior..."

"There is no need for that. But....if your conscience tells you...and you insist upon it, then, please, let me know and you can come visit me at work. Because of his injury, he's now teaching arts and crafts. But I am sure I can arrange something."

Suzanne was warmed by her father's understanding and unconditional support. She nodded, trying to hide her tears.

"Perhaps, Tuesday. I'll get the afternoon off. I can take the bus home before lunch…"

"Good. I'll come home. We'll eat together, and then we'll drive back to the hospital."

THIRTY-FOUR

From the first time she met him, Suzanne was impressed with the young prisoner who expressed his quest to learn about all things American. That night at the dance, she had been taken with the long fingers, the thin shock of sandy blond hair that dipped over one side of his forehead. Now, face-to-face without the threat of his being beaten up by her fiancé, she was lured into his deep Wedgewood blue eyes that smiled at her behind deep shadows of sorrow and pain.

"Someday, they will send us back," he said. "Eventually. I heard a rumor that almost all of us German prisoners are being transported to the countries Hitler's regime destroyed...to help repair the damage. Somehow, that seems fair...But I would be devastated if that happened to me."

"Why, Franz?" Suzanne asked gently. Sitting across from him at the crafts table, she boldly and uncharacteristically, yet instinctively reached out her hand to touch his. "Is there...?"

"My mother and...Greta," he whispered, opening

his hand to hold hers.

"Tell me..."

He explained in great detail about his mother; growing up on the farm without a father, and his admiration for Abram; the Gestapo searching first for him and then for all *Juden*; Greta and her lost family; and, of course, his great love of drawing and painting. He took off the canvas covering the easel behind him. When she saw the almost finished portrait in oils, she gasped.

"Have you shown this to my father?'

"Yes. Many times during the process of its creation. And that of its two predecessors. He has been most helpful in his guidance. He thinks it is quite good."

Having nearly finished the book the Reverend Fromüeller had given him, Franz expounded upon his affection and admiration for the founder of the Protestant Reformation, citing Luther's adamant objections to the immoral practices of the Roman Catholic Church. He cited references to the former monk's writings, his 95 theses nailed to the massive doors of the newly built All Saints Church in Wittenberg for all the world to see.

"He was conflicted and tormented all his life by his quest for principled morality, just like I am," Franz admitted, surprised at himself for bearing his soul to the young woman who looked so much like his girlfriend back home and who was so kind to visit him here. Looking into those dusty blue-grey eyes was almost as if he was explaining the painting directly to Greta.

"I wanted to show that. To depict in my portrait of him...his despondency, his abject loneliness...in his captivity...so far away from his family...of being so misunderstood even though he did what he thought was right."

Suzanne listened to what almost amounted to a lecture from a theology professor. She tried to remember what she had learned in Sunday school about Martin Luther. As Franz spoke so eloquently, she thought of Pastor Freddy's recent sermons on compassion for the detainees at Valley Forge and wondered how much he had inculcated this one with his own ideals.

"Have you learned all this from the Reverend Fromüeller?" she asked?

"Oh, *nein*. Not really...You see, he gave me this

book." He took D'Aubigne's volume out of his art supplies satchel and showed it to her. "And after I read most of it," Franz chuckled. "I was the one who taught him things he, a minister, did not even know."

Suzanne bristled at the German's hubris.

"Perhaps there were there things he had learned, but did not remember."

Franz considered this.

"*Ja*, perhaps. But he was amazed that I learned so much. As I told him, I grew up in the shadows of the Wartburg fortress where Luther stayed. And I know all the stories. Even the ones not in this book. When I am there...when I was there before the war...And now, reading about him, his very spirit seems to have touched my soul."

"Well, it certainly shows in the painting," she muttered cautiously. To her, the young man's lithe, slender build and kind eyes seemed to belie his streak of almost too assertive aggressiveness.

"Ah, then you, too, think it is good?"

"Oh, yes. Very good. Although, I am not that much of a judge of art...John...my fiancé...He is an artist, too. His brush stokes are very fine, very detailed. Uncannily very much like yours."

"Still....it is not a shame we did not – how do you say? – 'hit it off'."

"John has a very short temper. But it's very rare he does anything about it. He, and I, are terribly sorry about his outburst at the dance."

"And, yet, it is only you who have come to apologize."

"Yes, but you don't understand. He fought in, over Germany during the war and heard and saw things..."

"Things my misguided countrymen did?" Franz grimaced at Suzanne's nod, squelching his irritation at the blanket assumptions. "They are, were not me. Not me at all. I am different. I am, was against this heinous war."

"I agree, but...his, John's intentions. He was only trying to protect me."

Franz slammed the book down on the table, cracking its fraying, fragile spine.

"*Für Gott's Willen*, *Fraulein*! He knocked me down! A crippled prisoner who was only trying to get your attention!" He stopped to take a deep breath. "That, Suzanne, does not seem to me like he was protecting you, but assaulting me..."

Suzanne said nothing, waiting for Franz to calm down. As with John, she knew better at moments like this to say anything further.

"Then, I think it is your – what did you say his name was? – John?" he added through gritted teeth, "Perhaps it is he who does not understand…"

"Perhaps," she whispered. "But someday, he'll get over it. As I hope you will, too. And maybe someday, too," she offered, "you will meet each other again under better circumstances."

"No, I don't think so."

"Why not? He is, um, like you…a talented artist and," she inhaled deeply, "a very good man."

"Yes, maybe so. But…he is also going to be your husband. And for that reason alone," Franz finally sighed softly, taking her hand in his. "I don't think I want any further contact with *him*."

THIRTY-FIVE

Despite the altercation during their first meeting, Suzanne made it a point during the next few months, to visit Franz at least once a week.

She rationalized that his outburst was borne of his irritation of being summarily categorized and identified with all other Nazis. Deep down, she was still intrigued by what she was convinced was a gentle, kind soul hidden behind Franz's sad blue eyes. If nothing else, she would try to become a good friend and help him.

She took the occasional afternoon off from work, rode the mint green bus home, lunched with her father, and then afterwards drove back with him to the hospital to visit with Franz. Often, she and Abram attended the Saturday morning Lutheran services led in the small, squat prisoner's chapel by the Reverend Fromüeller.

And on at least four or five Sunday afternoons, she rode her bicycle to the complex. These were the best times, when she and Franz could sit almost alone near the victory garden enjoying the fresh, beginning-of-Spring breezes, chatting as they watched the various plantings begin to bud and grow.

During their subsequent visits together, neither one brought up John's assault at the dance nor Franz's singular explosion of frustration. She even offered to replace the damaged leather-bound copy of *The Life and Times of Martin Luther* with a new, cloth-bound one.

"No, *da bitte*. I like this one," Franz said, declining her offer. "It was Pastor Freddy's in seminary. That means a lot to me..."

She, too, like the reverend, brought him books from her growing collection of novels and biographies. When he asked for history books about the United States, she raided her father's crammed bookshelves, exacting a promise that Franz would not tell Abram and read and return the books as quickly as he could.

They discussed in great length his impressions about what he had read while he sketched his fellow prisoners working in the garden or the cluster of robins that had begun nesting in the hedgerow. Occasionally, he worked on the final sketches for his portrait, often commenting on why he used a color here, a few brushstrokes there to convey his thoughts and feelings.

She introduced him to her favorite authors, English as well as American: C. S. Lewis, whom he was slightly familiar with before the British theologian's works were banned and burned in Berlin as well as in Eisenach and Efburt; Dawn Powell, who fictionalized her beloved New York City in the 1930s; F. Scott Fitzgerald; and, of course, the great American humorist, Mark Twain.

Franz inhaled everything at a rapid pace, reveling in being able to read the great classics of Western literature in their original language. He also marveled at his new friend's breath of knowledge and broad literary experience for one so young.

Not only is she pretty, he smiled to himself, *and forgiving. She is also quite smart. And, she likes my painting. She will make a good companion and a wonderful mother.*

And although she was engaged to marry John and was, in fact, very much in love with the former gunner, Suzanne realized she was also growing almost inappropriately affectionately fond of the young prisoner. As time worn on, she had difficulty suppressing her feelings; finding it very hard to restrain from brushing the long, dark yellow bangs away from his eyes as he dipped his head over a book or one of his drawings, intent on catching a phrase's meaning or sketching just the right detail.

She had to catch herself more than a few times from looking too long into his eyes when they chatted.

What really lies behind them? she wondered. *Does he have the same feelings for me as I do for him?*

While John persisted in asking were she was the afternoons she had mysteriously gone missing from work or the Sundays she wasn't available to see him, she refused to tell him. Angry at first, John knew better than to press for any further answers. Suzanne was just as stubborn and determined as he was; if not, in her own way, more so. Suppressing his mounting annoyance, he bided his time knowing that eventually she would tell him why she seemed to be avoiding him.

She did, however, tell her mother why she came home for lunch so often and about her subsequent visits to the Valley Forge General Hospital, accompanied, of course, by her father. He had arranged the first few meetings until the guards and administrative staff knew that Suzanne, Mr. Kessler's daughter, could be trusted and allowed to visit on her own. Abram tried to dissuade his wife from thinking that Suzanne's being alone with Franz was nothing to worry about. Their daughter was not in any danger and her kindnesses toward the young, homesick prisoner were little more than common courtesies. Or so he thought.

"There is nothing going on," Abram explained. "If that's what you think...Nothing at all. Our daughter is very sensible."

"She'd better be," Katrina more than lightly threatened. She knew her daughter's gentle-to-a-fault kindheartedness; always trying to understand and reaching out to help others, despite their, or her, circumstances.

"We just spent a fortune on her custom-fitted wedding dress."

THIRTY-SIX

Peggy was the only one to whom Suzanne related her true feelings.

"You're, you know, playing with fire, girl," Peggy told her one evening as they sat in the living room of the small house on Washington Street. "Those prisoners are not supposed to be fraternizing alone with anyone from town..."

"We...he...Oh, for God's sake, Peggy! I am not fraternizing! And we are not alone. Half the time there are other prisoners around. Working in the garden or doing arts and crafts. And there are guards everywhere. And my father is sometimes nearby. You need not worry. There is almost constant surveillance."

"Half the time? Sometimes? Almost? My friend, if I were you, I'd remember that in less than two months, I have a wedding to be in...and break it off with that boy."

"There is nothing to break off," Suzanne protested. "He's...He's just a good friend. Well, maybe like a brother. That's all."

"That's all? I'd say, that's just about enough..."

Suzanne thought about what her best friend had intimated. *Am I really falling in live with Franz?* she asked herself. *Or is it just infatuation? The allure that he is a prisoner, was once our enemy?* She could still feel the gentle touch of his long, delicate fingers on her wrist as he returned a borrowed book or guided her to one of the park benches near the garden.

Certainly they are the hands of an artist. Are they also those of a sensitive lover?

She tried to shake the thoughts from her mind, torn between her love for John and their impending marriage, and her inordinately deeply heartfelt attraction to Franz.

"It seems...like I've known you all my life," Franz said one rainy late spring afternoon as they sat in a corner of the arts and crafts room. Two patients near the door were absorbed in building model airplanes; one was a B17 Flying Fortress, complete with two gun turrets, that reminded Suzanne of John's plight when he was shot down. She sank deep in reverie recalling her father's story the night she first met the young gunner.

"You have her eyes...and the same dark, curly black hair..."

"Huh? What did you say, Franz?" turning her thoughts back to him.

"You have Greta's eyes...very deep...the same blue-gray color...I could gaze into them all day..."

"Please, Franz, don't talk like that. Soon you will be shipped home. You will find her...and, well...Aren't you going to marry her?"

"I had planned to, but the International Red Cross says there is no sign of her. Nor of my mother. It would be useless to be shipped back and then try to find them..."

"I am sorry...But, you shouldn't loose hope. Or faith."

"Reverend Fromüeller says the same thing," he sighed, and then smiled. "But... you know, I could ask to stay here...and marry you."

"What?! That is impossible!" Yet, she briefly wondered if it was.

"Why?"

"It just is...That's all. I thought we were friends, Franz. Just friends. Remember, I am about to be married. So, let's leave it at that."

"I was just teasing," Franz said quietly, forcing himself to keep smiling. "It's just my way of saying how much I do like you...as a, um, friend. *Ein guter Freund.*" He took her hand in his, glanced up to make sure the patients did not see them, and brushed his lips over the top of her knuckles. "Yet...you will always, I promise, always be my American *Fraulein*..."

After that, afraid of her true feelings, Suzanne slowly decreased the frequencies of her visits, finally limiting them to just being with Franz after Saturday services; but only when her father and/or Pastor Freddy were nearby. Still not able to shake her deep affection for him, Suzanne hoped that by putting distance between her and Franz would lessen the intensity of her feelings.

When she finally told Franz she was really busy with the wedding and couldn't visit him as often as she did, he started to protest.

"But, you fill up so much my days of waiting...my thoughts of you...those eyes."

"Please, Franz. They only remind you of Greta's...Whom you really love."

"*Nein*. That is not true...How do you know I haven't come to love you as much? *Mein Fraulein...*" He bent down to kiss her cheek, but Suzanne, anticipating this, backed away.

"I can't hear any more," she said and turned to join her father and Pastor Freddy.

"I have to go now. Perhaps...I'll see you next Saturday. In church." Without offering any further explanations she walked away, hoping and praying that he would acknowledge and reconsider what she knew to be his false feelings and...understand.

As their nuptials approached, she spent more time with John, especially on Sunday afternoons. Listening to his stories, dreams, and aspirations for their life, and their eventual children, together distracted her mind from thoughts of Franz. She was coming to realize that despite her growing fondness for the talented and handsome prisoner, the handsome, kind, and thoughtful John was the love of her life.

Can I believe that this is really true love? She asked herself. *So, this is what it feels like.*

Even if he did have a short-fused temper, which,

she thankfully admitted, he had learned to control and that she was learning to steadfastly defuse, forgive, and forget.

Something, she realized, she might not ever be able to do with Franz.

THIRTY-SEVEN

"I am beginning to believe that all Americans are hypocrites," Franz complained to Reverend Fromüeller during one of his early evening visits.

It was late spring and the night air was warm, almost balmy. The pastor suggested they walk around the inside perimeter of the stockade. He listened carefully to the young prisoner.

"They say one thing when they mean another and then do a third something completely different altogether."

"We are not all like that. Some, most of us are honest. At least we try to be."

Franz related the conversation he had with Suzanne Kessler when she first came to see him.

"She came to apologize for her boyfriend and then averred her love for him. Yet she comes here often to see me. Without him."

"I know Suzanne very well," the minister said. "You may have misread her intentions. She is a very kind and honest person. In her heart, yes, she loves the young Mister Voight very much, but I know she is also quite fond of you..."

"But not in the way she acts toward me and how I want her to..."

"Then, you think of her more than a friend?"

Franz did not respond.

"Regardless of your feelings, it is unwise to fraternize with your captors."

"Ah, but she was the one fraternizing with me!" He paused, and then said, "But it doesn't matter any more. She has stopped visiting me by herself. I only see her when she comes to our Saturday services."

"Then you must put your love, er, your feelings aside. Move on, Franz. Soon you'll be able to return home to Greta..."

"If she is still alive."

"I pray that is so," Pastor Freddy said. Then, after a short, silent prayer, changed the subject.

"What will you do when you return to Germany," he asked.

"Find my mother, then resume my studies at the university. I want to be an ophthalmologist, like Doctor Harrup."

"And not a famous painter," the burly minister jested. "Or, perhaps, even a preacher...Like me?

You'd be a fairly good one."

"I doubt it," Franz chuckled. "*Nein*. No offense, but I have a fascination with the eye. How it works. How the retina captures light and transforms it into images. One's ability to see."

"One can see with the heart, too, Franz."

"Yes, but if one does not have vision, it is worthless."

"That is rather profound…"

"My father, like Luther's father, wanted me to be a scholar; a professor, hidden away in some small-town college. While I would like to emulate him…Luther…I can only follow his example of goodness and truth. Not the actions of his life."

He went on to explain that it wasn't only Suzanne that, although he thought he loved her, in whom he was disappointed. He cited a few of the Army MPs, including Lieutenant Quisling who was serving time in prison for his theft and assault.

"Especially Otto Kempf…"

"But, he is one of your fellow countrymen."

"Not any more. He escaped."

"I heard. But, still…

"He, too, was a hypocrite," Franz sighed. "I am

sorry, Pastor Freddy, but my time spent in your country has made me so jaded. I am trying, I truly am, like Luther, to find the goodness in all men, but it is a very difficult task for me.

"Especially when they wage wars against each other for no valid reason...And thousand of people are needlessly slaughtered..."

They had turned the last corner and had come to the point where they had started their stroll, near the long, low brick building that housed the camp kitchen and dining hall.

"I think," the minister said quietly, "that you are still quite young and even with all your experiences, you are still seeking to learn..."

"Yes, you are right. I have a lot to learn...And perhaps one of the lessons is not to be so judgmental...and not so hypocritical myself."

"Good lessons to start learning.. Ah, here we are, back again. Something smells delicious..."

"Three of our cooks were chefs in Leipzig before the war. Tonight they are roasting a pork loin with all the trimmings. Please, join us for supper."

"Yes, Franz, Thank you. I will enjoy that."

THIRTY-EIGHT

On a warm Sunday afternoon in late May, Suzanne suggested she and John take a walk in Valley Forge State Park. She made it a point to look her best, wearing a white opened collar blouse and a relatively short white skirt. Her stylish braided open-toed hourglass low-heeled sandals were just comfortable enough to walk in.

"You look, um, quite pretty, today, Susie," John said, opening the passenger door of the maroon roadster. "What's the special occasion?"

"Does it have to be a special occasion for me to dress nicely for you?" she asked coyly. "My darling fiancé; my loving husband-to-be?"

"No, I guess not. I'm glad I brought my camera," he said indicating the small brown leather case in the foot well. "I wouldn't want to miss taking a picture or two of you today."

Sitting on a small grassy hill after their walk, Suzanne carefully explained about her visits with and her feelings about Franz. She was mildly surprised and relieved when John showed no signs of annoyance or irritation.

"Why did you want to spend so much time with him?" he calmly asked. "Please don't tell me you really were falling in love with him..."

"To be perfectly honest, John, I thought I was. He fascinates, um, fascinated me. His stories. His talents...You should see his drawings, his paintings. The portrait he is painting. They remind me of your talent, John..."

"I really don't care to see them..."

"But...he is doing this oil painting of Martin Luther," she persisted. "The courtyard is very detailed. The fine architectural lines are something you would do..."

"I said I didn't wish to..." John's ire started to rise, but he stopped himself. "Sorry. Tell me more about this Franz."

"He is not like the other prisoners. He is kind...and lonely. And misunderstood. He just needed a friend."

"And you are, were that friend?" When Suzanne didn't respond, John slapped both hands on his knees and started to stand up. "Damn it, Susie. I have talents, too, as you so kindly have mentioned. And I am kind. Besides, he's a German, for God's sake."

"Yes, for God's sake!" she sputtered. "Lest you forget, John Joseph Voight the Second...So are you!" She lowered her eyes and then whispered. "And so am I."

John pondered this for a while. It was true. Both their parents were first generation emigrants. While naturalized American citizens, they both were the grandchildren of foreigners; of Germans. They both, especially himself, should be more understanding of the plight of their former countrymen trapped against their wishes under a cruel regime and a cruel, power-hungry warmonger and then behind American barbed wire while he, Suzanne, and their families were free.

He tried to put himself in Franz's place, to feel his feelings. But he couldn't. In his mind, the young prisoner who had so captivated his fiancée's heart and mind was still "the enemy". And that thought, even more so, stopped him from feeling any further compassion.

John sat back down beside Suzanne and took her small, soft, tender hand in his. Oh, how he loved that hand!

"Okay. Point well taken. But still..."

Again she realized deep in her heart that even with her infatuation with Franz Weberhardt, Suzanne could never really fall in love with him. Not in *that* way. Nor as much or as deeply as she already was with John. It was Johnny, she was sure, smiling as she realized she had relaxed her rules of propriety, that she really wanted to marry.

"Oh, John. Don't be jealous. I am not seeing him anymore. It's you I truly love," she whispered, enclosing his hand in both of hers, rubbing his slight, short fingers already gnarled from his arduous work at Kessler and Gulden and his own painting endeavors.

"Please believe me, Susie. I'm not jealous. I'm just concerned. About you. Your safety. You mean the world to me, Susie. The whole world. If anything should happened to you...Well, that's all...I..."

"Honest, John," she quipped. "I *love* you! *Only* you! Never forget that."

"Good," he said. "Cause I was just about to return the fancy-dan tuxedo I rented."

"Not until after our wedding."

"Well...alright, then," he smiled and then leaned

in to kiss her.

Suzanne Elizabeth Kessler and John Joseph Voight the Second were married at Bethany Evangelical Lutheran Church on June 1, 1946.

The Reverend Frederick Yohan Fromüeller presiding.

THIRTY-NINE

Toward the end of May, 1946, Colonel Henry "Hank" Beakers received orders from the United States War Department that all prisoner of war camps were to be closed and the remaining prisoners repatriated back to their countries of origin. The majority of the German soldiers, as he had learned earlier, were to be first sent to those countries decimated by the *Wehrmacht* during the war. He had Captain Templeton inform the prisoners.

"Why?" Franz asked, saddened by the news that the rumors about the fates of the prisoners were true. He was eager to return to Eisenach to find his mother...and Greta. "If we, I were to be sent to reconstruct, rebuild the remnants of the countries my, those Nazis destroyed...That will take years! It will be an eternity before I'd be able to go home."

"Sorry, my son," Pastor Freddy said, trying to console him. "But those are the orders and we, you must obey them."

"I will escape, run away..."

"You would be shot for desertion."

"There is no longer any Germany army to desert from..."

"There are now orders to shoot any prisoners who dare to escape, Franz." The Lutheran minister thought for a while, trying to come up with a solution to Franz's dilemma. "But, there might be a way..."

"What? Anything! I must get home..."

"There are schools being set up to teach a few German prisoners...the tenets of our government, our democracy, and a bit of American diplomacy. Those who attend are to help with the rebuilding and revitalization, the rebuilding of your own homeland...

"I could try and arrange it to get you sent to one of them. It would delay your departure from the United States by only a few weeks. And, soon afterward, you would be sent straight home, to Germany, soon after. It would not take months or years, as you so dread."

"And the real purpose of *Diese Schulen*...these schools?"

"To assist our troops, our government in

reconstruction of Germany's government. To help it become a true democracy. You would be teaching your fellow citizens...the wisdom and your knowledge of our country and its culture. And you have the advantage of being able to speak English. You'd be an asset to the cause."

Franz frowned as he contemplated the possibilities.

"*Würden Sie dies für mich?*

"Well, they are accepting only twenty-thousand...out of the four hundred thousand of you that we've played host to," Reverend Fromüeller smiled. "There are such schools up and down our east coast. But as a member of the Lutheran Commission for Prisoners of War... I think I can get you into one. I will try and do that for you. "*Ja. Ich denke, ich kann es für Sie tun.*

It was all Franz could do to contain his excitement. Hardily shaking Pastor Freddy's massive hand in gratitude, Franz was convinced that he would give the kind minister the painting he had just about finished.

No one else, not even *Herr* Kessler, deserved it more.

The next afternoon, Franz carefully carried the finally finished portrait of Martin Luther at Wartburg to the wood-working shop across the pathway from the arts and crafts building.

He had learned that the older infantryman, whose severe and painful facial burns were finally healing, was training to be a carpenter while recuperating.

The once suicidal patient would be the perfect craftsman to make a rustic wooden frame for the painting.

FORTY

On the last Saturday of services, a week before he and the rest of the prisoners were to leave the VFGH complex, Franz presented the framed portrait to the Reverend Fromüeller.

"In thanks for all your help, Pastor Freddy," Franz said, trying to keep from crying. "Please, remember me."

"You are very generous, Franz, but I do not deserve this. There were others here that helped you more than I did…"

"*Nein*, it is to you I want to give it. When I finally return to Germany, I will think of something else to send back to *Herr* Kessler and his…family."

"But I didn't do anything to deserve this…"

"*Nein*! I shall hear no more. You were there, here for me….You arranged for me to go to one of the special diplomacy schools in upstate New York, D'Aubigne's biography of Luther…the search for my mother. For Greta…Shall I continue?"

"Okay, okay…I get the point."

"Not to mention your services," Franz rambled

on, "...and your enlightening sermons. Visiting me in the hospital. Taking care of Manheim..."

"Manheim?" Pastor Freddy feigned surprise. "What have I done for him? He rarely attended my services...let alone..."

"You somehow found out his true identity and had the Red Cross in Germany see to it that he could practice medicine when he returned..."

"Oh, that," the reverend said humbly. "How did you know? I thought it is a Christian's duty to keep one's alms a secret, lest I lose part of my eternal reward."

"Manheim, er, Samuel is Jewish. So it doesn't count," Franz laughed. "You welcomed us both...us all. Tried to make us feel at home...And even if it is thanks just for that, the painting is my gift to you."

"Okay, then. I accept. I will hang it in my study at home. And, someday, young man," he said, gently giving Franz a warm Pastor Freddy bear hug, "you'll come back and see it hanging there for yourself."

FORTY-ONE

Otto Kempf and Jimmy Watts kept their first but constantly changed their last names and lied about their true identities as they travelled back and forth across the northwestern United States looking for work and a place to settle down. After two months of drifting, they finally found employment on a large commercial farm back in Wisconsin. They told the elderly owner, Giuseppe Petruccio, that they had lost their Social Security cards and licenses when robbed on the road by a "gang of young hoodlums".

The kindly Giuseppe accepted their story without question, grateful to have the extra help, especially when he discovered that Otto was adept on tending – and killing – pigs and making sausage. The former *Oberfeldwebel* was settling in, returning to some semblance of his roots. Before being conscripted, he was a simple, robust farmer in the German countryside who raised pigs and cows and made his own locally renowned brand of liverwurst, sausages, and gruyere cheese.

Otto tried to teach Jimmy the art of curing,

cooking, dicing, and spicing the meat before stuffing it into casings made of porcine stomach linings. But Jimmy, ever the union organizer, was not interested. He wheedled his way into the old farmer's good graces and began to boss the other farm laborers around. Giuseppe was delighted that the two former vagabonds were great workers. Giving them more and more responsibility meant that he could spend more and more time with his large family.

"I will-a gibe you assistance...for your new social cards," he said late one afternoon. "Then I make-a Jimmy here a foreman and Otto I put in charge of the pigs." He was not concerned about Otto's shallow knowledge of the English language. Many men and women in Wisconsin were of different nationalities and many kept to their "old ways". It never dawned on him that his two now favorite employees were an escaped convict and a prisoner of war on the lam.

When they heard of Germany's surrender and the final end of the war, Jimmy decided to leave the bucolic life of working on a farm and headed back home to Bayonne, New Jersey, to reunite with what was left of his family and to contact his former employer.

"Here's hoping I can get my old job back," he grinned, shaking Otto's hand as he prepared to leave. "Sure you don't want to come with me? You could go back to Germany..."

"*Nein*. I like it here," Otto said in his still broken English. "Now that you have taught me about America...democracy, I think this is my country. There is nothing for me to go back to. America is now my home."

"Okay, then," Jimmy said, "Suit yourself." He waved goodbye as he walked down the dusty dirt road toward the highway to catch a Greyhound bus back East. "Take care of ol' Petruccio!"

"*Ja!* That I intend to do!"

Six months later, Otto married Giuseppe's oldest daughter.

"She certainly is a homely thing, but a good worker," Petruccio chuckled when Otto asked for Maria's hand. "You are welcomed to her." After the wedding, Otto became a partner in the farm and, when his father-in-law passed away, the owner.

He became, of all things, a model citizen of the United States, even running for and winning a position on the town council. Finally shunning his pro-Nazi tendencies, Otto Kempf even, at his wife's insistence, joined the local church which just happened to be of the protestant Lutheran denomination. He thought of the burly, bear-like minister who first tried to impress upon him the need to hold services in the VFGH prisoner camp.

Now, wouldn't he be amazed? he smiled, remembering Maria's words when they first walked arm-in-arm into church together.

"God only knows what you've done in your past, Otto," she had chided. "to make your soul so much in need of peace and salvation...But I am glad you are here with me."

He squeezed his wife's hand as he escorted her into the narthex.

Oh, lieber Gott... he chuckled to himself. *If she only knew...*

Years later he took his small family back east to Pennsylvania to celebrate his adopted country's Bicentennial. On their way to Philadelphia, *Herr* Otto Kempf, now Mister Otto Kowalski, insisted on stopping at the VFGH complex which was now hosting soldiers wounded in the Vietnam conflict. He walked brazenly into the main administration building and handed the receptionist a huge bouquet of yellow roses for the nurses and a large box of chocolates for the patients.

No one, as he had expected, knew who he was. Nor did he tell them.

He smiled as he left the building, wiped a drop of snot from his nose, and began to whistle "Lily Marlene."

FORTY-TWO

Before dawn on the morning of June 19, 1946, nearly sixteen long months after he and 249 others first arrived at the prisoner of war compound at Valley Forge General Hospital, Franz Weberhardt turned on the pathway leading out of the barbed wire fencing and took one last backward glance at Barracks 3. The now very worn leather satchel containing art supplies that Tommy had given him was slung over his shoulders. He clutched the wooden case of well-used tubes of oil paints and horsehair brushes Abram had shared in one hand and the newly carved handle of his walking stick with the other.

"I am taking along with these," he said out loud, leaning heavily on his cane, "*Viele Erinnerungen, gute wie auch schlechte.* Many more bad memories than good. But yet, I will remember the good ones more."

He made a brief stop at the engineering tool shed, hoping Herr Kessler was there, but it was, he knew, a bit too early for him to start work yet. Franz did not have the luxury of time to wait. The buses and lorries taking the prisoners to the Phoenixville train station were going to leave in less than an hour and he still had two more stops to make.

He left the large manila envelope containing the long letter he had written and the charcoal sketch he had made the night before of the two furnace towers overlooking the stockade on Abram's workbench. His engineering mentor and friend would read the words of thanks later. *It is best this way. I really couldn't handle all the emotion. But,* Franz promised himself, *I will write to him once I get back to Eisenach.*

He then went up to one of the orthopedic wards to find his fellow prisoner.

"You're not going with us?" he asked his friend, Manheim, now officially *Herr Doktor* Samuel Goldberg.

"They've made arrangements to let me stay on...at least for a while. I am perfecting a new method of fusing shattered bones so they can knit back together. There are hardly any good facilities left standing in Europe in which to finish my work. If I am lucky, I can become a citizen here and then bring my family over..."

"I wish you well, Man...er, Samuel. I will miss you and our little chats." He was surprised when the doctor hugged him close and softly whispered a few words in a guttural language Franz could not understand.

"I am not sure what that means...But coming from you, it has to be good."

"*Darauf achten. Gott möge sie sicher in seinem Herzen, bis wir uns wieder treffen.* It is an old Hebrew blessing...I just made up."

Franz laughed. Samuel was once again up to his old verbal tricks. "I will try and take care," he said. "But as for being safely in God's heart...I'll keep the faith and just leave up to Him."

"See you soon, Franz."

"*Ja. Herr Doktor. Sehe dich bald.*" As he started to walk down the corridor away from the orthopedic ward, he heard Samuel mutter, "And take care of that leg. It took a great deal of my knowledge, talent, and energy to put it back together."

Since it was Wednesday, Franz knew that Pastor Freddy would not be in the chapel, let alone on the hospital grounds. Instead, he slowly hobbled up the steps of the administration building and left another large manila envelope for the minister with the receptionist. Then he asked to speak with Colonel Beakers.

"You did all you could to be kind to us...to help us," he said, shaking the hand of the Chief Medical Officer. I am sorry about Lieutenant Quisling and all the trouble I caused you..."

"It's all in the job," the colonel said distractedly, chewing an unlit cigar. "You weren't any trouble...At least you aren't any more now. You'd better hurry...Your bus leaves soon."

"Thank you again..."

"Good luck in diplomacy school. I know you'll do well," he clipped. The prisoners were finally going. The compound in back of the complex was to be closed and eventually razed to the ground. Now he could get back to the real business of running an Army hospital.

With a lot on his mind and in a hurry to meet with Captain Templeton, Beakers left the reception area and hastened into his large corner office before Franz had a chance to walk out the door.

As the buses and lorries carrying the prisoners

drove out the hospital complex's back entrance, an old dark blue Chevrolet station wagon with wood-paneled doors sped up Charleston Road. Reverend Fromüeller had hoped to catch up with Franz Weberhardt before he and the other prisoners left the compound. He wanted to say goodbye and wish him...Well, not all the best. That would not be the right think to say, considering the circumstances.

He had a telegram in his jacket pocket from the Lutheran Commission on Prisoners of War. It had been delivered to his home just a half-hour ago, detailing the results of the International Red Cross search for Gwen Weberhardt and a young Jewish girl, "supposedly" named Greta Hornweitz. Pastor Freddy wanted to break the news to Franz as gently as he could in person, but as he pulled up to the small prisoners' chapel and saw the last of the convoy disappearing up Township Line Road, he knew he was too late.

No, no. Perhaps it is not too late, he thought, turning right onto the main road that would take him into town. *It is never too late! I'll catch him at Penna Station.*

As the convoy wended its way up Bridge Street, past the Bridge and Main Street bus stop on that unusually warm beginning-of-summer morning, Franz watched out the opened bus window hoping to see Suzanne standing there. But less than three weeks ago, his young American *fraulein* had married her "Sergeant Johnny". Franz doubted he would ever see her again, but he wanted so much just once more to gaze into her bright, kind blue-grey eyes that were so much like Greta's. *Bitte, lieber Gott. Nur noch einmal.*

As his bus approached the corner, he thought he saw her familiar face. She was sitting in the front seat of a maroon roadster, watching as his bus went by. *It has to be her,* he wished. *There is no such thing as coincidence...I know...It is her.* He waved out the window, calling her name. But the traffic noise and the unmuffled roar of the convoy engines drowned out his shouts.

Just as the bus was about to pass them, the young woman turned away to look at the young man in the driver's seat.

Someday, Franz sighed, smiling inwardly to himself as the convoy headed toward the train that would take them to Camp Shanks, New York. From there, after the process of repatriation, he would immediately travel on to the training school in Saratoga Springs. His fellow ex-prisoners would eventually board a troop ship bound for Europe.

Someday. I promise. I must tell her that. Someday, I will return.

FORTY-THREE

As they did every day after returning from their brief honeymoon in Washington, D.C., Suzanne and John rode to work together in his, now their shiny 1935 Ford Roadster. Stopped at the light where Main crossed Bridge they heard the rumble of large trucks and buses lumbering up the street on their way to the train station.

"Looks like the last of the prisoners is leaving us," she sighed. As they passed, she scanned the lorry beds, hoping to catch one last glimpse of Franz, not realizing that this time he might be in on one of the buses.

"Yes," John said, taking his wife's hand in his. "The war is, now, finally over."

She turned from the passing convoy to fondly gaze into her husband's dark brown, compassionate eyes. They had been happily married for less than a month, but Suzanne Elizabeth Kessler Voight had a premonition that she would remain so to John Joseph Voight the Second for at least the next seventy years. Consumed by her love and thoughts of her future life with John, she did not see nor hear the young artist waving and shouting at her.

FORTY-FOUR

Delayed by red lights and early morning rush hour traffic, he reached the station just in time to see the last of the German prisoners hastened by MP guards aboard the Pennsylvania Railroad passenger cars. Their idling steam engine seemed impatient to continue its journey.

"Only passengers allowed, sir," one of the two conductors said as the Reverend Fromüeller tried to board the train in search of his young friend. "Please step behind the line."

The brawny pastor had no choice but to remain on the station platform and watch in frustration as the train began to huff and chug its way north. He angrily crumpled the telegram in his hand, dismayed that Franz might never know the fate of his mother and Greta.

After almost a year of hiding Greta on her farm, Gwen's deepest dread had finally come true.

Die Gestapo und braun-shirted Storm Troopers made another sweep of the Thuringia area around

Eisenach, hoping to round up what they hoped would be *Die letzte der Juden*. Acting on a tip from the local dry goods store – apparently Frau Weberhardt had not paid her outstanding bill in two months – they invaded Franz's home in search of more of the last of the Jews.

The two women crouched covered in hay and straw under the altar, mistakenly thinking that the determined soldiers would be careless and lazy enough not to find them. But urged on by a promise of extra rations of food and a bottle of beer each for each *Juden* found, they were more than diligent.

It was a young, eager *Soldat* freshly recruited out of *Hitler's Jugendbewegung* who heard a lamb plaintively bleating in the barn where he discovered the two women.

"*Hier! Hier! Ich habe Ihnen*!" he shouted, kicking aside the wooden stanchions and clumps of straw. He pointed his machine gun at Gwen holding the frightened Greta in her arms. "I've got them!"

Finally caught and arrested, they were transported via cattle train to Poland. It did not take the camp authorities there long to decide what to do with *Der junge jüdische Mädchen* and the woman who had traitorously harbored her.

According to the now-crushed telegram in Pastor Freddy's hand, members of the American liberating troops had discovered the names of *ein mutter und ein Junge jüdische Mädchen aus Eisenach* listed in the meticulous files that the Germans kept of those interred in Auschwitz.

G. Weberhardt and *G. Hornweitz* had been crossed out with black slashes, indicating that they had been eliminated.

FORTY-FIVE

Franz mounted the station stairs and slowly headed to one of the three the train cars assigned to the prisoners of war. He was deeply saddened that he could not, once again, command Suzanne's full attention.

"No matter," he quipped out loud. "I'll catch her sometime in the future."

With hope in his mind and trusting faith in his heart, he boarded the Pullman and settled into his seat as the lumbering steam engine slowly chug-chugged its way out of Penna Station, pulling him further and further away from his recent past as a prisoner and toward his future, to be, once again, a free man.

Staring out the dusty, streaked window at the passing Pennsylvania countryside, he questioned, despite what he thought were honorable intentions, if his promise to "someday return" after he found his mother and his beloved Greta, would ever really come true.

FORTY-SIX

Later that morning, a dejected Reverend Frederick Yohan Fromüeller sat in his study trying to draft a poignant sermon for next Sunday's service. Pausing to reflect on the Biblical passage he had selected to preach about, he glanced up at the young prisoner's portrait of Luther at Wartburg Castle that now hung over the stone-front fireplace.

He thought back on the past sixteen months and reflected on his friendship with the young, talented prisoner who wanted nothing more than peace and to return home to his mother's farm.

Pastor Freddy was despondent that he was unable to give Franz the news of his small family before he boarded the train. Concerned that the young talented painter might never get over the grief and sadness that would surely overtake him.

I wonder, he conjectured, *when he finally does return home...*

What ever will become of him?

EPILOGUE

He walked with a prominent limp, supporting his left leg with a silver-handled, white rubber-tipped mahogany cane. His once curly, unruly stock of sandy blond hair was nearly gone. A light, thin fringe of dull yellowed gray graced over his ears, the back of his head, and draped down the nape of his neck.

It took him a few slow, agonizing minutes to walk from the taxi cab to the concrete sidewalk and then up the six marbled steps of the red-bricked Harrup Hall administration building which once housed the offices of the Post and Camp Commanders and the hospital staff. It seemed all so clear to him now, as if it was just yesterday and not almost sixty years ago when he had hobbled up these very same steps – finally a free man – to say good-bye to his friendly captors and to leave a letter for the kind Lutheran minister who had taken a personal interest in his talents and ambitions.

Ach! Those were the days! he thought, smiling through his dull pain as he navigated the last of the steps to the stark white front double doors that led into the lobby and reception area. Before he could reach one of the handles, the doors were quickly opened by two eager energetic young men. *Probably students*, he surmised. *After all, this is a university now…*One of students held the door for him as he inched his way through and crossed the plush green and brown carpeted floor.

"Welcome to the University of Valley Forge," the woman behind the reception desk smiled. Wisps of thick, curly salt-and-pepper hair framed her face. Her eyes were a soft, dusty grey. "How may I help you?"

He grinned as he gave her his name in the thick German accent that had never left him, even after being fluent in English and an American citizen for nearly forty years. Nor had he lost his gentle, beguiling hubris. He smiled at the name plaque on the desk. "Franzine". *Of course,* he thought as he shyly smiled back. *She with the dusty blue-grey eyes would name one of her children after me.*

"I have an appointment with the, um, the president?"

"Yes, Sir. I believe he is expecting you. Please

have a seat and I'll email him that you are here..."

"Thank you. But actually, Franzine," he whispered. Not forgetting the good manners his mother had instilled in him, he nodded slightly, trying to suppress a chuckle as he said her name. "But it is *Doktor*. Ph.D. Ophthalmology."

"Ah, yes. Doctor..."

He nodded again in acknowledgement, then turned and made his way to a worn brown leather couch under a bank of high windows. With great difficulty, he lowered himself onto it. His arthritis, eventually resulting from the injuries sustained during the beating was acting up again. *Probably due to this cold, northeastern weather,* he surmised. Once settled, he rested his hand-carved wooden cane against his leg and then surveyed his surroundings.

A medium-sized painting, framed in ridged, fading gold-tinted wood, hung over a small credenza along the light grey wall across from him.

In it, a young man dressed in a late 17th Century long red robe slouched against a large, leafy tree that shadowed what looked like the walls of a castle. He held a small book in front of him, but was glancing away from it, staring thoughtfully across the courtyard. A small bevy of doves fluttered at his feet.

"Aha! So this is what has happened to you," he laughed out loud.

"Something wrong?" a kindly, deep baritone voice asked as Dr. Don Meyer stridently crossed the foyer to greet his long-awaited guest.

"*Nein*...no, no! Something is actually right," the elderly doctor said, nodding knowingly at the painting. "I remember painting it...Martin Luther at Wartburg Castle. So vivid is my memory of every moment, every brush stroke. Just as if it were...yesterday.

"So," the university president smiled. "The story, then...It really is true."

AUTHOR COMMENTS

This novel is based upon true facts surrounding the incarceration of 250 or so prisoners in a small compound on the campus of Valley Forge General Hospital. Some of the incidents related were culled from extensive research and incorporated into the story solely to give an authentic feel for the camp atmospheres and lives of 400,000-plus prisoners of war who were held captive in more than 511 PW camps maintained by the United States Department of War across the continental United States. Some dates and minor facts, however, have been changed and appropriately altered to fit the story's varied plot lines.

The real portrait of "Martin Luther at Wartburg Castle", painted by a German prisoner of war during his stay in the stockade at VFGH, is signed with the initials "F.W." It now hangs in the office of the Associate Director of the Storms Research Center on what is now the campus of the University of Valley Forge, just outside the borough of Phoenixville, Pennsylvania. The painting's faint, meager history formed the basis of *The Prisoner's Portrait.*

Luther at Wartburg was donated in 2014 to the University by Mary-Louise Smith, the youngest daughter of Reverend. Frederick Wilheim Flothmeier, once pastor of St. Paul's Evangelical Lutheran Church in Norristown,

Pennsylvania. The minister, who was fluent in German, came to preach to and worship with many of the German prisoners during their 18 month stay at Valley Forge.

Who "F.W." actually was is currently unknown.

While fictitious, many of the characters presented themselves to me as the literary avatars of real people, including residents of Phoenixville, who lived here during World War II and who were more than helpful as they extensively related their memories. A few unselfishly provided me with invaluable pictures, photographs, and lengthy oral historical accounts.

The Reverend Frederick Yohan Fromüeller is an amalgam of the Reverend Flothmeier and Reverend Nevin E. Miller, who was the retired pastor of St. John's Lutheran Church located between Jackson and Starr Streets. Because they spoke fluent German, both were able to provide worship services for as well as comfort to the PWs at VFGH during their incarceration. My humblest apologies to their families for taking liberties with their real, sterling characters for literary purposes. However, I hope my "Pastor Freddy" embodies the deep and abiding goodness and prevailing faith of them both.

Contrary to the fictionalized account of Herr Otto Kempf's disappearance and a misinformed article that appeared in *The Phoenix* in 2002, no German prisoners of war escaped during their confinement at VFGH. According to one guard, John Knapp, "Why would they? They had it so good..." Thus the expression, "the Fritz Ritz", which I liberally took from Krammer's seminal historical account. However, James "Jimmy" Watts is based upon a real United States Army soldier who was court-martialed and attempted to escape from federal prison. He sustained burns during this endeavor and was sent to VFGH to recover. He did, in fact, escape during his stay. Despite a week-long, all-encompassing man-hunt by both local authorities, a cadre of U.S. Army MPs' and the FBI, he was never found. His back story in this novel is pure speculation.

Although there was a myriad maze of underground tunnels – as well as above-ground corridors – that connected the original 182 hospital buildings, most of them collapsed when the buildings were torn down to convert the 180-acre campus to that of Valley Forge Christian College. A few, however, still remain intact; although they are now sealed off from public use. They are, according to Stan, one of the current maintenance engineers, "pretty well preserved, but very eerie".

The characters of Suzanne Elizabeth Kessler and John Joseph Voight the Second are based upon two dear friends and tennis buddies who lived, loved, and married in Phoenixville during the trying times of World War II. While based upon fact, their stories and personalities embodied here were highly fictionalized to represent any number of young couples across our country who encountered German prisoners.

The last of the German prisoners of war held captive in over 511 prisoner of war camps in the continental United States departed on Tuesday, July 23, 1946 from Camp Shanks in Brooklyn, New York for Europe on the troop ship *Texakana*. The majority of those held in the compound at Valley Forge General Hospital were on board.

The hospital was eventually closed in 1974, after serving military wounded throughout the Korean War and the Vietnamese conflict. The campus was finally granted by the United States Government to the Northeast Bible College in 1976 and was renamed the Valley Forge Christian College. Affiliated with the Assemblies of God, it became the University of Valley Forge in 2014, under the tireless, expert guidance of its current president, Dr. Don Meyer.

Hopefully, in telling these stories of what happened on the now prestigious university campus during those fateful eighteen months between February 6, 1945 and June 19, 1946, the events will never be forgotten.

June J. McInerney
November 2015
Phoenixville, PA

ACKNOWLEDGMENTS

My sincere thanks, first of all, to Lucy Sanna, author of *The Cherry Harvest*, for first writing the story of German prisoners of war held in Michigan during World War II. Her seminal novel was an inspiration

After reading it and passing it along to my dear tennis buddy, Betty Weber, she hardily suggested that I write my own novel about the prisoners of war held captive at Valley Forge General Hospital. I am most deeply grateful to her for her encouragement, continuous moral support, and for telling me her many anecdotes about herself and her family living in Phoenixville during World War II.

Thanks also to Peggy Yeager who related to me childhood memories of Reverend Miller and singing in the Phoenixville High School Choir for the VFGH patients and staff at the USO hall in downtown Phoenixville. Thank you, too, for all the doggie treats!

Gratitude also goes to all those whom I've met along the way and who literally "came out of the woodwork" to share their stories and experiences, including an elderly graduate student whom I coincidentally met one brilliant summer afternoon outside the tennis courts. She graciously provided me with a three-degree-of-separation link to one of the actual prisoners.

I also thank Sue Marshall and Jack Ertell, members of the Historical Society of the Phoenixville Area, for their help, encouragement, and provision of articles about the prisoners of war in Phoenixville.

I also owe a debt of gratitude to Dr. Don Meyer, president of the University of Valley Forge who lent me the inspiring biography, *The Life and Times of Martin Luther* by H. Merle D'Aubigne. He and his lovely wife, Evie, have been most supportive during the process of writing and publishing *The Prisoner's Portrait* and, as a result, have become good friends.

Lastly, but not least, my humble and most grateful thanks go to Julia G. Patton, the Associate Library Director of the Storms Research Center of the university, who not only eagerly suggested authoritative historical books on WWII prisoners of war in America, but also shared her own personal research materials culled from back issues of *The Forge*, the VFGH in-house publication; and *The Daily Republican,* the local Phoenixville newspaper of the time. Thank you, Julia, for all your help and for first telling me the story of the iconic painting that now hangs in your office. Thanks, too, for finding me the UVF baseball cap!

But, most importantly, I give prayerful thanks to "F.W."

Whomever and wherever you may be.